JACK IN THE GARDEN

A Jack of All Trades novel

DH Smith

Earlham Books

Published 2021 by Earlham Books
Book design & cover art by Lia at Free Your Words
(*www.FreeYourWords.com*)

Text copyright © 2021 DH Smith

ISBN: 978-1-909804-46-3

Chapter 1

Jack pushed the wheelbarrow across Wanstead Flats, the clouds closing in. What was the point of continuing? He stopped and let go of the handles. There would be no seeing. Not now, or any time tonight. Why carry on? His usual site was 200 yards further in. What could he do there with this cloud cover? Or here, or anywhere else. Or ever. He just knew he couldn't be at home. It had taken all his reserves to get out of the door. Under the sky, with the telescope, his troubles would shrink in the immensity of the heavens.

That was the hope.

Now he watched the clouds obliterate the last pinpricks of light, the moon long gone. There was no one else in the darkness of the Flats, not even a dog walker. A few copses of trees here and there, sensed rather than seen. He knew where they were, waymarkers, to the clear area of football pitches where he would usually set up his telescope.

When there was something to see.

At the fringe of the Flats were street lights and car beams; light pollution that would have annoyed him but tonight he didn't expect anything else. Bring on the rain and lightning, fire and brimstone. Cue the Four Horsemen of the Apocalypse.

Jack was broke. In debt up to his ears, and about to get worse. If he didn't pay his trade bills, which he couldn't, wholesalers wouldn't deal with him. The word gets about quickly.

And the mortgage was always there at the end of the month.

A millstone round his neck. Three months behind. He had been ignoring the letters, expecting payment for work to come in. He was used to robbing Peter to pay Paul. Some late payment would usually come in. Self employment was like that. But this time! The second time in a year he'd been clobbered by a client's bankruptcy. Hardly recovered from the first, and now hammered by the second, as if the gods had picked him out in their game of dice.

Money was on the way, Baldwin had told him repeatedly. In a few days, some stock dealing to be sorted out. Be patient. Just a few days, always a few days...

And down came the guillotine. On his neck.

By text, can you believe it? Three terse sentences, scored into his brain: *Sorry, Jack. There is no money. I am bankrupt.*

He'd rushed round to Baldwin's office. Baldwin wasn't there, but the bailiffs were, taking everything of value. They didn't know where he was. Didn't matter to them. Jack left them carrying furniture and computers to their van. And spent hours in the afternoon phoning, to be told repeatedly: 'leave a message after the tone'. He'd left a dozen.

At last he'd got through. Baldwin had told him it was true. He'd lost everything. He was sorry for what he owed Jack, but there was nothing he could do. He didn't have a penny. Luckily, the house was in his wife's name. At that point Jack had rung off. He had no wish to hear about Baldwin's luck.

Jack was owed close to three thou. Which he could forget. Baldwin made that clear, between apologies. The first in line was the tax man, then came the banks. There'd be peanuts by the time they got down to Jack.

The one bit of luck, irony of irony, he didn't have the cash to get drunk. Not quite equal to Baldwin's luck. All he'd eaten today was toast. His doctor had told him to eat more fruit and vegetables, or he risked making his diabetes worse. Fat chance. Decent food was a dream. The menu was all but blank.

How was he going to surface? He sat on the edge of the wheelbarrow. To get work you need cash, working capital, while you await payment. And then there was his flat. The mortgage ringing its demand like a plague warning. It kept coming back to that. He'd be out on the streets. Nothing he could say to the mortgage company. Scrooge was its patron saint. Widows and orphans bundled out the door. No sob story would wash. Pay or pack your bags.

He'd sleep in the van, but if it wasn't insured it was illegal on the road.

Tomorrow, he had a date. That was a joke. He smiled at the thought. Computer dating, set up when he'd still been expecting payment. Penny, her name. An apt name, considering. They'd arranged to meet at a pizza place in Stratford. Baldwin had assured him he'd get cash today. On his honour. How could that scumbag string him along like that? Week after week. How could he have believed him?

Better cancel the date. How much credit did he have on the phone? Jack couldn't think straight. Was that hunger weakness or the fuzz of misery? He wondered how many others Baldwin had pulled down as well as himself.

What to do first?

A hole was clearing in the clouds. Wasn't that Vega in Lyra? It had to be. There. A corner of the Summer Triangle. Close by would be the Ring Nebula. He'd only ever seen it as a red smudge. Was it worth setting the scope up? Screw the mortgage. Let tomorrow do its worst.

He scoured the clouds, the clear patch was growing. That had to be Deneb in Cygnus.

Worth a try.

Rapidly, he unwrapped the telescope, taking off the blanket that he used to protect it in the belly of his van bringing it here. This wasn't his usual stargazing spot, he'd given up before getting there. The ground was a bit rough, but it would have to do.

He set up the three legged mount as firmly as he could, and carefully attached the scope, every half a minute or so glancing up at the sky to make sure the hole of sky was still there. If he could see the Ring Nebula tonight, maybe it would bring him luck. Not that he believed in astrology, or anything like that, but he needed luck. Tonight was a night for crossed fingers, lucky rabbit's paw (not for the rabbit), wishing upon every star, planet and comet...

He was adjusting the focus on Vega, when the man came.

'Hello, Jack. You're not easy to find out here.'

A deep, friendly voice. Jack couldn't make him out in the darkness. Just a silhouette of a tall, broad man with a voice he didn't recognise.

'Do I know you?' he said warily.

The man flicked on his phone. By its light Jack saw a black man in a well-cut grey suit, short hair, clean shaven, a large manicured hand holding the phone.

'I'm sorry,' said Jack. 'I don't know who you are. Should I?' Questions buzzed in his head like angry bees. 'How do you know me? How did you know I was here?'

'My brother told me,' said the man, keeping the phone alight. 'He said you often went out on the Flats with your telescope. He'd gone out there with you one time.'

'And your brother is?'

'Nick Baldwin.'

'That lowlife.' Jack could see the resemblance now. Both tall and broad, this man better tailored, younger. The same features. 'Your brother screwed me. Did he tell you that? Led me along. I've been working for nothing in his shop. Buying materials, piling up debts. And he's gone bankrupt on me.'

'I know. I'm sorry.'

'A lot of good that does me.' Jack peered at him. 'You're not in business with him, are you?'

'Lord God, no.' He flashed out his hands in denial. 'I wouldn't work with Nick if he was the last man alive.'

'So what are you doing here?'

'I know you're in trouble.'

Jack said nothing, trying to make sense of this encounter on the Flats in the dark of night. Something was coming. What?

'I have a job offer,' went on the man.

'Forget it,' said Jack instantly. 'I've had more than enough of your family.'

'Cash,' said the man. 'Strictly cash.'

This alerted Jack. Cash counted. Cash was holy.

'For what?'

'I want a kitchen island. Made of bricks. Can you do that?'

'Yes,' he said. A reflex, though he'd never done one before, but how difficult could it be? 'Have you got plans for it?'

'I have,' he said. 'But I haven't brought them with me.' He smiled. 'This didn't seem quite the place... Tomorrow, I'll show you.' He held out his hand. 'Ace Baldwin.'

Jack took it with some reluctance. 'Jack Bell.' He might have withdrawn quicker if the shake hadn't been so firm.

'Cash, you said?' The man nodded. 'How much? When? What about materials?'

'I've got the materials. Bricks and mortar. They're all at the house. The plans too.'

Jack screwed his eyes, trying to make out more of Ace's shadowy face. 'Hang on, not so quickly. I don't get this. Fine, you've got the materials. But you seek me out, past eleven o'clock at night on Wanstead Flats. Sure, I'm a builder, but I'm not the only one. Why me?' He paused an instant, searching the man's stance, his suit, the cut of his

5

hair as if there might be hidden clues. 'Why didn't you just phone me?'

'I tried several times. You were continually engaged, or the phone was off.'

'That's how I lose work,' said Jack. He knew why he'd been hard to reach today. First he'd spent the best part of the afternoon and evening trying to contact Nick, then he'd turned the phone off to avoid his own creditors and give himself time to think. 'Usually,' he added, 'clients don't come searching for me.'

'You have another quality I'm looking for.'

'Apart from being broke?'

'I am sorry about that, Jack. I really am. My brother takes dreadful risks. He should be jailed as far as I am concerned.'

'Let's take that as read. But this other quality... What's that? Can't be astronomy.'

'No, not astronomy. I have heard you've done some detective work... Worked with the police.'

'Who told you that?'

'Hayley.'

'Who? I don't know any Hayley...'

'Hayley Amis. Detective Constable Hayley Amis. Tall woman. We're in the same martial arts club.'

'Hayley.' He nodded as he recalled her. 'I wouldn't call us friends. She works with my mate Fayyad.' Jack stopped, getting back on track. 'So you want a detective builder. Not a lot of choice there.' He half laughed. 'But here's one in front of you. Sort of. So let's get the whole story. I know about the brick island in the kitchen. You've got the materials and the plan. All well and good. What's the detective work?'

'I want you to keep an eye on my wife. She works from home, so while you are there...'

Jack held up his open hands. 'I don't do that stuff.'

'I thought you said you were broke.'

He was, he most certainly was. And this man, who happened to be a Baldwin, not a good reference, was offering cash. Somewhat dubious cash, he suspected. But cash.

'How much?'

The man laughed. 'To the point. The heart of the matter.'

'I'm not working for nothing again. How much?'

'Five hundred pounds to start with. In cash.' Ace put his hand in his jacket pocket and brought out a slim bundle of notes. 'Ten fifties here. And then three hundred a day...'

Jack sucked his lower lip. Big money. There must be a catch to this. He did a quick calculation. Two thousand by the end of the first week... Got to be dodgy.

'What do you think your wife's up to?'

'That's for you to find out, Jack. You want the job?'

Ace held out the bundle of cash. Jack hesitated for a second or two, then took it.

Chapter 2

Back home, at the sitting room table, he counted the money, as if it might be transient cash, about to be sucked back into the seventh dimension. He had, after all, wished upon a star. And money had come. Mind you, he'd done that before and none had come. Which proved you can prove anything if you're willing to ignore what doesn't fit. Though, why Deneb or any other star should give a fig for his troubles...? But then again, none of this worked on logic.

He had 495 quid, that's what mattered. He'd bought some fish and chips on the way home. Real money on the table. Jack couldn't stop looking at it. He'd had trouble changing a fifty in the chip shop. They'd held it up to the light to examine the watermark, went through a list of forged numbers before reluctantly accepting the note. Quite a transaction. He had nothing else to give them. Couldn't pay on his maxed out credit card.

Tomorrow, bright and early, he was to meet to meet Ace at his house. 8 am to be exact, and he would be there. The house was only up the road, opposite that community garden with the fancy mural of flowers and birds on the fence. He'd never been inside. Flowers weren't his thing, but 500 pounds was. Most definitely. He could become quite the miser. All in fifties too. The man in the fish and chip shop was annoyed that Jack was cleaning him out of change.

So good to have money.

Ace had got his number alright. Cash. They say every man has his price. His had been cheap enough. The question was, what would he have to do for it? Build a kitchen island. Nothing questionable there. He'd sussed that one out. Ace said he had plans for it. But, big glowering but, Jack had to watch Ace's wife. Watch her for what? A lover? Most likely. Or something else. No point guessing. Tomorrow was tomorrow.

The detective builder goes on shift.

He'd pay all but one of the fifties into the bank tomorrow. Let it clear and pay it towards his mortgage debt. Dare he go on the date tomorrow night? It was only a pizza house, and he could keep his bill down to under a tenner. But she might be one of those who expected the man to pay. And no way could he do that.

Some other time maybe, when he was in the black. But not tomorrow. He'd text her. In fact, do it now. Of course, she might be in bed. It was, after all, nearly midnight. But it mattered, and he needed the right answer to the question he had in mind.

I've been having an argument with a friend. He says the man should always pay on a date. What do you think?

He looked it over before pressing 'send'. It implied that he disagreed with the mythical friend. True enough, he did. He pressed send.

He had options now. If she didn't reply by tomorrow afternoon, he'd cancel. He wasn't taking the chance. If she replied saying the man should pay, he'd cancel too. He reflected on what he was deciding. Was it really all down to money? It was, at this point in his life. Bottom line, he could spend a tenner max, and that would not cover both his meal and hers. She might be the next Miss World, but she had to pay her way.

Jack laughed. The condition he was setting hardly made him a good bet, though it was unlikely Miss World would be computer dating. Still, it mattered how you begin. Alison, his ex, when they'd been dating her, she had always paid for herself. Paid for him too from time to time.

Though, that was different, once you got to know each other. It was expecting to be treated from the start that wasn't right.

Suppose she was broke too. Suppose she had just lost her job. Suppose her boss had just gone bankrupt.

Suppose the moon was green cheese.

A text came in.

Tell your friend, a woman should pay her own way. This is the 21st century. See you tomorrow. Don't be late.

That was telling him. She had opinions. Had she sussed there was no friend? You could never tell with a text. Bald words. He read it again. What information did it hold? She would pay her own way. This was the 21st century, and she didn't like people being late.

So far, so good.

Chapter 3

He drove to Ace's place. Not that it was far, less than two hundred yards, but Jack kept his tools in his van, and you never knew what would be needed. He parked in the road by the house in front of a black BMW. Ace's? He'd bet that it was. A man who could hand out five hundred in cash wouldn't go for cheap wheels.

It was warm and dry; the sky clear and blue. Tonight would be much better for observing the Ring Nebula. But he was going on a date. Penny. In Stratford. Always nervy, first dates. You don't know what to expect. You're being judged. Held up to some perfection which you don't know.

And he'd be doing the same. Perfection would derail them both, him and her, if that was the guide. Grades of imperfection then. Move down the scale. How much allowable. No wonder people got married, just to stop the constant appraisal.

Except it didn't. Human beings judged all the time. Sizing up, sizing down. Ideals of beauty, of fashion, race, class. All the time considering what other might think of your thoughts, your choice of food and drink, your clothes, face, body. Who could be free in this zoo of judgement? Not a man bought for five hundred. He'd dropped three rungs in ethics overnight.

In the drive was a stack of red bricks. A handsome colour, almost apple red. Leaning against it, like buttresses, were sacks of mortar. That saved hassle as he wouldn't be needing to make up his own with sand and cement. Probably best for a small job, less waste.

Less sweat too. With his diabetes, he was always looking for ways to ease the effort. Fresh fruit and veg, he had the money now. No excuses. Though, no doubt he'd find some.

He hoped Ace had the quantities right, both for bricks and for the mortar. Not a problem for now, but latter in the job. If he over bought, that was fine, if under, at least Jack couldn't be blamed.

That BMW had to be Ace's. He'd moved it to make room for the materials. Had to be.

The house was a semi-detached Victorian villa. There were stairs to the front door which was behind a proud, cream portico. There were three floors and a newish red-tiled roof. One floor was half below ground level with stairs going down. Did someone else live there, or was that Ace's too? There were three central bay windows, one above the other, for each floor. The plaster work was cream and in good shape, as were the fiddly bits that the Victorian liked: mock pillars at the windows, and classical supports under the sills. All pukka, redecorated in the last year or so.

Although, he'd met Ace, Jack could tell as much about his client from the externals of the house. More so perhaps, as a house didn't lie. The front garden had been covered in flagstones, alternate lines of pale red and white. There were tubs with red, yellow and blue flowers. Jack had no idea what they were. Flowers, he could tell you, colourful, neat. You want to know more? Ask a florist, not a builder.

All in all, it said a decent income, someone who wants to impress. A good sign for a jobbing builder. Unless it was all built on stretched credit. But he was getting paid in cash. No risk of bouncing cheques, no dubious promises, and no materials to buy, so if Ace went bust, Jack would not be one of his creditors.

He must get to the bank, and pay off what he could of the mortgage. Urgent. Before they sent out the bailiffs. Jack recalled those at Nick Baldwin's yesterday carting off the

TV and computer, and could almost spare an ounce of sympathy, except the house was in Baldwin's wife's name.

Jack went up the stairs and through the portico, and rang the front door bell. He was a few minutes early, important today as he was meeting Ace to have the job explained. And meeting the wife too, the one he'd be watching, though how on earth he'd be doing that he hadn't thought out. If you are laying bricks, you are laying bricks, you can't be watching who is at the door, what she is doing with whom in her bedroom.

Play it by ear, take the money, and deal with the surveillance however he could.

Did she have a lover? Why else do you watch a wife?

Ace opened the door.

'Ah, come in, Jack. Ready to work I see.'

Jack was in his paint-splattered blue overalls and t-shirt contrasting with Ace's light blue suit, white shirt and red tie. Certainly smart. Jack wondered what he did. To pay for the house and BMW. And give him 500 in cash.

Jack followed Ace through the hallway. Coats on hooks, a woman's bike against the wall, doors on either side. There were stairs going up, and further along stairs going down, presumably to the basement rooms.

At the end of the hall was the kitchen. Ace led Jack through. The room was large, the width of the house and about as long as wide. The back wall had a high window, above the worktop and white goods. showing greenery beyond. On the left of the window was a door to the garden. Under the window, in turn, a dishwasher, a double sink and a fridge. Along the right hand wall was an oven and hob, a row of wall cupboards, and a freezer. A metal rail suspended from the ceiling went the length of the room on which hung pots and pans from s-hooks.

The centre space in the room was empty. A middle-aged black woman was frying at the cooker. She was over-weight, with a full bosom and weighty arms. She was wearing blue slacks, too tight at the hip, and maybe weren't when she bought them. Her hair was grey and black and she wore no make up.

'My mother,' said Ace. 'This is Jack the builder who was working for Nick...'

'How do you do,' she said abruptly, and then ignored him completely, going back to her frying. She had a Jamaican accent unlike her son who was definitely a local. 'Did you need to take the table out, Ace? Where on earth are we to sit and eat?'

'There's the sitting room.'

'Food will be cold by time I get it there.'

'You could eat on the patio.'

'I might just. You could have put the table over there.' She indicated the side wall.

'But not with mortar dust and bricks. It's bad hygiene.'

'Hygiene, smygiene. I'm going away in a week. You could have waited. And with Mo here too. It's so inconvenient.' She turned to Jack. 'How long are you going to be?'

Jack opened his mouth to answer a question he couldn't answer, when Ace intervened.

'I haven't explained the work yet, Mum.'

'Then hurry up then.' She sighed heavily and looked to Jack. 'You would think he'd consult his own mother. But oh no. Not Mr Ace Baldwin.'

Ace rolled his eyes, half turned away so his mother couldn't see.

'Well, go on then,' said his mother. 'Tell him what to do or he'll never be done.' She turned to her frying. Jack could smell salt fish and onions.

'The island is to go here,' said Ace, indicating a space parallel with the cooker and cupboards. 'There was a table and chairs here. Removed so you can work.'

'Yes, removed alright,' said his mother turning over the fish in a swish of boiling oil. 'Last night already. He never discusses a thing. Just does it. No wonder he makes enemies.'

'So the brick island is here,' went on Ace, trying to ignore her. 'It will have a green marble top. That'll be coming in a day or two. Six stools are on order.'

'Stools!' exclaimed her mother. 'We are to perch on stalls as if this is a night club.'

'The island will function as a breakfast bar and a worktop,' said Ace, concentrating on Jack in the face of the interjections.

'Smart,' said Jack, imagining the island and stools in place.

'The window frames will be painted red to match the bricks, as will the door to the hall and garden door. I'm sure you can manage that.'

'Save the painting till I'm on holiday. Please!' exclaimed his mother, putting out plates. 'What's with all the rush? I just don't understand. Anyone would think you were going to die tomorrow.'

'No problem with painting,' said Jack. 'And we can delay it if you wish. You have the plans for the island?'

'I'm ready, Dad,' came a call.

A young lady had come a little way into the room. Her hair was short, her complexion dark like her father's, she had purple lip colour. She was wearing jeans and a red t-shirt, with smart leather sandals on her feet.

'Morning, granny. Dad's always late. Makes me late.'

'He was born three weeks early,' said his mother, 'so he's always late to make up for it.' She paused, screwed up her mouth in disapproval as she stared at her grand daughter. 'Why you not in school uniform, girl?'

'It's dress down day, Granny.' She threw out her hands. 'Come on, Dad.'

'Won't be long. Wait in the sitting room, Sally,' said Ace. 'I'm explaining to the builder about the island.'

'And I'm going outside to the patio to get some peace.' His mother deliberately crossed between Ace and Jack with her tray on her way to the garden door.

The young woman sighed. 'I'll be late again.'

'Wait in the sitting room. And don't argue.'

She shrugged and left.

Ace blew out his cheeks once she'd gone. 'This place can be a mad house in the morning. At least my brother doesn't get up till noon. My other brother, Mo. I'm sure you'll get to know the whole family very quickly. Right. Let me show you the plans.' He took out a file from a drawer in the units, and removed a paper. 'Here we are.'

He handed the paper to Jack. It was a plan of the room, with the units, the white goods and the area of the island, all with dimensions. On top of the plan, in red, were the words Acebal Developments.

'Acebal your company?' said Jack.

Ace smiled. 'It is a town in Argentina. International connections.'

Jack mused. 'I don't know about Argentina, but I do know you are Ace. 'And 'bal' is the first three letters of your surname, Baldwin.'

'Smart fellow. You're the right man for the job. Enough about my company name. What do you think of the plan.'

Jack was looking it over. 'Well, I can see how where the island fits into the kitchen. That's clear. But there should be another plan...'

'Correct. Here's the plan of the island itself.' Ace handed him a second sheet, showing the island from the top and from the side, again with dimensions.

'This is excellent,' said Jack looking over the drawing. 'Professional. From Acebal Developments, I note. Did someone from work do it for you?'

'No, no.' Ace smiled, pleased by the praise. 'I trained to be a surveyor. I was always good at technical drawing. Good spacial eye. I drew it up. Any questions?'

Jack could see it how it worked. Where the island went, and its construction. All he had to do was build it. And then more work in the offing with the painting of doors and woodwork. All cash in hand.

'Yes, I know what to do,' he said. 'Excellent plans, a lot better than most.' Glancing at the drawing, he added. 'One thing though. What is the island to sit on?'

'The floorboards.' Evidently surprised at the query. 'Isn't that OK?'

Jack wasn't sure whether it was or not. But he was the builder. Act the part.

'Plastic sheet, I think,' he said thoughtfully. 'Mortar could leach out weakening the floorboards.'

Ace scratched his head. 'As you say, as you say. Minor problem. Put some down.'

'I've some in the van,' said Jack. 'No problem.'

The bell rang. Once, then again. Then full on and blasting.

'What on earth is going on?' exclaimed Ace. 'Some mad delivery man at the door...' He called into the hallway. 'See who is at the door, Sally.' He turned to Jack. 'I think we have more or less wrapped this up.'

'Yes,' said Jack. 'The material in the drive, got the plans. I can get going.' He looked about furtively. 'And the other business, your wife...'

Jack was cut off as a man rushed in, in shirt sleeves, hair awry. Jack knew him at once. His former employer, Nick.

The man screamed at Ace. 'You let me go down the tubes. You bastard. You pulled the plug.'

Jack took a step back, getting out of the way. This was a family row. He'd had way too much of Nick yesterday.

'I couldn't let you go on, Nick,' said Ace, standing his ground. 'You were throwing good money after bad.'

'All I needed was a few days. You wouldn't even give me that.'

'It wasn't my call...' began Ace.

Nick leapt at him, grabbed his brother's shoulders and attempted to wrestle him to the ground. In a swift move Ace pushed Nick's arms up, stuck out a leg, pushed Nick over it and felled him. Instantly he was on top of him, holding Nick down.

'Get him off me!' yelled Nick, wriggling like a beetle on its back. 'Call the police. He's crazy...'

'Calm down, man,' said Ace, his full weight on Nick, knees on his shoulder.

Sally came running in.

'Get him off me!' yelled Nick, arms waving. 'Call the police!'

Their mother rushed in from the garden.

'What is going on here!'

She grabbed Ace's arms. 'Get off your brother. You hear me! Off him now!'

Ace eased off. Nick thrashed out, punching his brother on the nose and into his eye. Ace yelled, rose, holding his nose, blood trickling through his fingers.

'I'm going to be late,' exclaimed Sally to no one in particular.

'Catch the train,' Ace managed to say. 'I'm in no state...'

Sally ran from the room.

Nick was crouched on the ground, his face in his knees, sobbing.

'The two of you should be ashamed of yourselves,' their mother yelled, addressing one then the other. 'You are brothers. This is family.' Then more gently to Ace. 'Come, come. Let's clean you up.'

She lead Ace from the room, holding his nose, blood seeping through his fingers, leaving Jack with his former employer.

Jack had kept out of the fight. Ace could clearly handle himself, with his martial arts. He'd only got hurt when he eased up on his brother. Nick appeared to be unhurt physically, but emotionally a wreck. Jack, though, was hardly the person to soothe him.

'Him, my brother of all people,' moaned Nick, his face in his knees, 'he got them to pull the rug.'

Jack couldn't help some sympathy. Yesterday, he'd wanted to throttle him, but today was today. And he had money. So he could afford a little pity.

'What am I going to do? My wife's gone. I'm going to lose the house.'

'I thought it was in her name.'

'Both our names. Did I say something else? I don't know what I'm saying half the time.'

A lie for all seasons. Jack knew that too well.

'The receiver has been called in,' went on Nick. 'I don't know what they are going to leave me with.' He looked up at Jack. 'I would have killed him, you know.'

A very partial view of the fight, with Ace sitting on his chest.

Nick wiped a hand over his eyes. 'Jack oh Jack. Sorry to involve you again.' He half smiled. 'Bet you rue the day you ever met me.'

'I'm OK,' said Jack. 'I'll manage. You have to calm down. You've got take advice.'

'I'm finished.' He was talking to the floorboards. 'My wife's gone. We had the mother of all rows. She's taken the kids. I don't have a brass farthing.'

His mother had come into the room.

'Would you believe it?' she exclaimed throwing up her arms. 'Ace has gone off to work. Washed his face, changed his shirt. And out the house as if nothing has happened.' She walked around the space, shaking her hands in disbe-lief. 'All he can think of is work.' She indicated Nick on the floor. 'Both my sons, both crazy.'

'I'm going to lose the house, Mum.'

'They'll take a few months before they get round to it,' she said. 'I know this. We lost our house with your father's gambling. It'll be all lawyers now. I know. And it's half hers, lots more sorting out. Busy, busy, taking ages passing papers to each other Where's Anne and the kids?'

'Gone to her mother's in Harlow.'

'You can't go home on your own. Alone in the house. Not in this state. You'll have to stay here. You boys, always fighting. You and Ace.' She signed heavily, the weight of the family on her shoulders. 'Let's go in the sitting room. Jack has work to do.'

She helped Nick to his feet. He stumbled weakly, the walking wounded, as she helped him leave the kitchen.

Chapter 4

Jack marked the perimeter of the island with masking tape, relieved to be alone after the family hullabaloo. He'd been a bystander. Yes, he'd lost money yesterday, but that was another Jack in a faraway universe.

Today, he was in work with money in his pocket.

Nick was being calmed down by his mother. She'd come back into the kitchen and made tea, offering Jack a cup and then returned to her ministering. Leaving a quiet space. Family away, just him and work to get on with.

A job he'd come into blind. Accepting it out of necessity, even though he'd never built a kitchen island before. But the plans were clear and he had the materials on hand. The island marked out, it was time to lay bricks. He needed tools from the van, and the plastic sheet for underlay.

All straightforward.

A woman came into the kitchen. She looked down at the masked off area. Ace's wife, he guessed, a black woman, her hair tied back. A full figure, no make up, wearing a pink t-shirt and jeans, her feet bare.

'You must be the builder,' she said.

He nodded. 'I'm Jack.'

She held out her hand, he shook it. Business like.

'Nadine,' she said.

'Are you Ace's wife?' he asked, in case she wasn't.

'I am for my sins.' She half smiled. 'I wait until the door slams twice before I come upstairs, but this morning there was such a racket. What's been going on?'

'Nick had a fight with Ace.'

'Who won?'

'No one. Nick's in the sitting room with his mother, miserable as sin. Ace got a bloody nose and maybe a black eye, but he's gone to work anyway.'

'He would. What about Sally?'

He felt rather like a noticeboard. Maybe she should be asking her mother-in-law. Then again, he was the least involved. And part of his job was to keep an eye on the woman in front of him. Easier if he was sociable.

'Is Sally the schoolgirl?'

'That's the one. My daughter.'

'She's gone in by train. Dress down day, she says. In a panic that she'll be late.'

'Not uncommon,' she said. 'You must think this an asylum.'

'It was half an hour ago.'

'My husband is a control freak. And his brother's gone bust.'

'Nick is blaming him for it.'

He was wary, watching her. Nadine was his quarry. However had he agreed to such a chore?

Money.

'I've no idea if my husband is involved in Nick's bankruptcy. Ace's finances are a mystery. He's got his fingers in so many pies. But he's got you here to make *his* island, that much I do know.'

He noted the stress on 'his'.

'You don't approve?'

'Why does it have to be made of bricks? Answer me that,' she said fiercely.

'They're not usually,' he said cautiously.

'Of course not. Most of them are wood. They have drawers and space underneath. This will be just a brick box in the middle of the kitchen. An idiotic, empty box with a marble top.'

'Didn't you discuss it?'

'We don't talk. We shout.' She laughed, strolling around the masking tape on the kitchen floor.

He should be working. Then again, she was work. He should keep her talking. She might say something useful. Not knowing he was the eyes and ears of her husband.

What a dirty job.

She crossed the kitchen, and took the electric kettle to the sink and filled it. 'We are divorcing. This is his house. I live in the basement flat for the time being. There are inside stairs for me to come and go.'

'You don't have a kitchen downstairs?' he said.

'There is a kitchen. Well, a room.' She had put the kettle on and was spooning coffee into a cafetière. 'But there's no cooker, no fridge, and so forth. Just a sink. I use it for my studio. So I come up here when the door slams in the morning. He works late in his office most nights, which is a good thing. The least we see of each other the better.' She turned to him. 'I am assuming you want a coffee?'

'Yes, please.'

As Ace owned the house, Jack mused, he could do what he liked to the kitchen. He was on his knees, pretending busyness, looking at the plans on the floor. His wife could rage to kingdom come and it would make no odds. But there had to be more to it. Sure, the island would have no drawers, but this was a big kitchen with lots of storage space. So why all the anger?

It came to him. The island showed his power over her. He wouldn't change a thing, because he didn't need to.

Top of the class for that. But he'd better take care.

She had her back to him as she made the coffee, going from foot to foot as she got cups, plates and biscuits from the cupboards. Attractive, quite a figure, all that hair, alive in her anger.

'How does parenting work?' he said, pretending he wasn't looking her over.

'With blood, sweat and tears.' Her back to him as she stirred. 'Sally goes up and down my stairs. To me, to him. He spoils her. Rowing parents are bad for kids, you know.'

'I've got a 15 year old,' he said. 'We did our share of rowing. But we don't live together.'

'Lucky you.' She turned to face him. 'I want you to ask you something. And please be honest.'

He was expecting her to ask about his relationship with his daughter and ex. Instead, she said:

'Has he asked you to keep an eye on me?'

He hesitated, a beat too long.

'No.'

She was watching his face intensely. He had to look away.

'I don't believe you,' she said. 'You wavered before answering.'

'I was surprised at the question.'

'I know my husband. We have been married over 18 years. I know how he operates. I believe he asked you to keep an eye on me. You being in the house, him being at work. He doesn't trust me. Not at all.'

She half smiled, as if waiting for an answer. To a question, he had already answered. What else could he have done but deny his watching brief.

'I need to start work.'

He rose, began walking to the door to fetch tools and materials.

'One moment,' she said. He turned at the kitchen door. 'Swear to me he hasn't paid you to spy on me.'

'I swear.'

He had gone too far to say otherwise.

'Swear on your daughter's life.'

'This is ridiculous. I've done enough swearing. I've got to get my tools.'

Jack strode off, down the hallway.

'How dare you walk out on me!' she yelled.

He stopped, he couldn't leave things like this. What a scene, what a family! He turned and came back into the kitchen.

'I'm just here to do a job,' he said. 'Please, Mrs Baldwin, let me get on with it.'

She faced him across the kitchen, hands on hips, her bare feet firm on the floor. It was obvious this would happen. He couldn't spy. He wanted to tell her. Admit he was a penniless idiot who'd taken on a job he knew was beyond him.

'I'm here to build an island,' he said weakly.

'You are. I believe that much. But that's not the end of it. My manipulative husband wants a spy in the house. And it's you.' She pointed him out as if there were a jury present. 'Judas.'

Jack didn't reply. Any words would incriminate him. As would silence.

'What does he think I'm up to?' she said, as she crossed to him.

He held his ground. Being by the door he had to or he'd be in the hallway.

'I don't know what he thinks,' he said. 'I, I...' he lost his words.

She poked him in the chest several times. 'You don't know a lot. Do you, Jack?' She laughed mirthlessly. 'You're a lousy private eye. I bet you haven't even a camera. Not even wired. You're way out of your depth here.'

And then, without warning, she took his hand in both of hers, and bent it backwards, eager to hurt. As if through him, she was hurting her husband.

Jack swung her round to get his hand free, but she held on. They were clasping both hands like best friends in the playground, swinging round and round. Jack jerked to a halt, pulling her to a stop.

She let go. He could see her seething, watching him, watching her.

'Your brother in law owes me three thou,' he managed to say. Hardly knowing why he was telling her this or anything. 'Left me with a pile of debts.'

'You and half the world,' she said. 'His wife phoned me. She's left him, taken the kids.'

They were staring at each other. Her eyes deep brown and liquid, high cheekbones, smooth skin, mouth slightly parted. They were breathing in unison.

'I was desperate, Nadine.' He wanted to repeat her name, but it would say too much. 'I was working for Nick until yesterday. He texted me, saying he'd gone bust. I was in a hole, going to lose my flat, and God knows what else. But your husband turned up and offered me a job. To build an island in the kitchen.'

'And to spy on me.'

'Yes.'

There. He had admitted it. Jack blew out his cheeks in relief. She put a hand to his chin, then slowly moved the fingers to his lips.

'What are you going to tell him, Jack?'

He held her fingers. The fight had gone out of them.

'That I can't do it.'

'No, no, no. You can, Jack. Most certainly you can. You need the money, fair enough. You will tell him exactly what I am up to.'

'And what's that?'

She looked down the hallway as if someone might be there.

'Come downstairs,' she said quietly. 'We'll have our coffee down there. Give me five minutes, get some tools or something, come in by my street door. I don't want his mother catching us talking in the kitchen. She must have heard me yelling anyway. She'll get back to Ace. Come downstairs. I'll show you my paintings. We'll concoct a tale.'

Chapter 5

Jack was on the patio, outside the kitchen, with the island plans on the cast iron table. It was hot, even with the sun behind the house. The back garden was parched, a third of it in shade. There was a lawn with flower beds at the side, then a low hedge and over it, he could make out, runner beans and a shed beyond them.

Not his territory, gardens. Fine to sit in, but he didn't know a dock from a dahlia. Not that anyone ever asked him. Nadine had offered to show him her vegetable patch and herbaceous border, but he'd excused himself, saying that he had to get working. She'd opened the house side gate for him, and he'd brought out tools from his van.

He hardly saw her paintings. She'd let him in via her downstairs street door. They'd embraced in the hallway, and gone into her studio. She'd closed the blinds. A little hand holding as they sipped coffee. Footsteps upstairs held them back. Another time, not here. It kept them half honest, she to her estranged husband, and he, well he was dishonouring the bargain, but he could say he needed her to talk. They would go further, he knew, well beyond explanation. But not here. Not with her mother-in-law over their head soothing Nick. Nadine assured him that she never came down as now they didn't speak.

'That being the case, let me be what she thinks I am,' she'd said. 'Though don't rush me, please.'

The implication was step by step. Not here. She was the sort he fell for, full figure and enthusiastic. It was energy that made her hot. Difficult to get back to work. Coffee and a little hand holding, a brief kiss when he'd left, not much, but mental turmoil. He'd hardly done any work. Heart and head pounding.

It would happen. Jack attempted to excuse himself. Husband and wife were divorcing. He wasn't breaking up a marriage. It was already broken.

And what might it lead to? Nadine and himself. Nowhere. Somewhere.

All the complications in this family and this job.

He must work. So hard to turn off, head buzzing with futures. Work. He stared at the plans. They were something of a blur. Work. He'd left her in her studio painting. Now work. Still the demon. He rose, stretched, looked into the blue of the infinite sky. He had a job to do, a roof to keep over his head. A kitchen island to build, and he hadn't laid a brick.

Jack looked at the plans. Clearer. Lines and numbers. They made sense, but something was bothering him. Nadine hated the very idea of the island, but it wasn't that. Though, he did hope she wouldn't give him grief over it.

'It's why I am here,' he'd said. 'The island.'

'That's its only advantage,' she'd replied.

She didn't like it, but she didn't own the house, nor was she paying him. Put that to one side. The niggle was the island itself, which he'd barely had time to think about until now. What with all the fuss, and the Nadine interlude. It had began to come as he was laying out the area of the island on the floorboards with masking tape. He'd suddenly thought: I wouldn't start from here. Ace wants a brick kitchen bar. Fine, he was the customer. But it didn't need to be full bricks as the only load to be carried was the marble top. It could be just be slip bricks which were slivers of brick, about a quarter thickness. They would be stuck on wooden panels with mortar run between, screwed to wooden uprights. And the end product would look exactly like a brickwork island.

Except that was out. Ace had already bought the bricks and the mortar. So this was going to be the real thing. Bricks, though, were heavy. And this was his concern. The length of the island would rest on three or more joists. That should be OK. But the two ends would need to rest on a joist too. Surely?

Ace hadn't considered the full weight of the island, and only now had Jack caught up with the job. Not his fault, well not totally. He'd only found out the details of the job when he arrived. Then the fight, then Nadine. That interlude was his fault. His mind had not been on the job, it had to be admitted. But it was now. More or less.

So, step one, find out where the joists were. The flooring was varnished floorboards. They would be screwed to the joists, so he could find the joists from the nail heads and see if Ace had placed the island correctly.

Having cleared this up, Jack was about to leave the patio and go into the kitchen to do his check, when a man came out carrying a tray. He had a mass of Afro hair in disarray, and a grubby white t-shirt featuring three black men on an Olympic rostrum, their fists in the air.

'Hi, man.'

He smiled broadly, and placed the tray on the table opposite Jack. He held out his hand. Jack shook it, a little uncertain whether he should or shouldn't.

'I'm Mo. The one they don't talk about.'

Had Jack heard of him? His head was all over the shop with who was who in this household.

'Jack,' he said. 'Doing the work in the kitchen.'

'I've heard too much about that.' Mo laughed. 'From Ace, from Nadine, from Mum. Man oh man!'

He laughed and sat at the table. Before him was a plate of toast and a black coffee.

'Take as long as you like, Jack.' he exclaimed. 'Don't mind me. I'm not your boss. Make a big mess, annoy 'em all. That's fine by me.'

'You're Ace's brother?'

'Yup, you got me. I'm the little one. 'cept I'm 35, and not so little no more.' He counted on his fingers. 'There's Nick, he's the oldest and even more stupid than me. Gone bust. You know that?'

'I do.' He had no wish to explain his involvement. But wondered whether Mo knew about the fracas between his elder brothers. Big house. Mo on the top floor maybe. Perhaps he didn't.

'Number two is big shot Ace,' went on Mo. 'He's up in stratosphere.' Mo pointed way up in the sky.

'What's he do?'

'Property dealer.' He crunched into a slice of toast. 'Buys, sells. Never builds anything. Just buys, waits for the price to go up and sells on. It's a nice little racket. Perfectly legal, but a racket.'

Jack agreed silently. He wasn't going to badmouth his employer to his brother.

'You live here too?' he said.

Mo chuckled. He had a couple of teeth missing in his front uppers, making his grin quite piratical. He could do with a shave. Or maybe he was growing a beard. It was at that uncertain stage.

'That's a cute question,' he said. 'I've been here four months or so. Ace wants me to go. He doesn't like my life-style. Says it is a bad example. I say, worse than property dealing!' Mo threw his head back, laughing at a vision in his head. 'Oh man, that wasn't wise, saying that to brother Ace, bastion of capitalist freeloaders.'

'You said that too?'

He sniggered at the memory. 'And a few more things. With Ma and Sally in the front row. All so shocked.'

'What was the comeback?'

'Ace called me a parasite,' said Mo sniggering. 'But tell me,' he leaned forward, wiping away the grin, 'who is the worst?'

'Not my place to decide,' said Jack, not knowing any details of Mo's lifestyle to make the comparison.

'Wise man, keep out of family affairs. But I know you agree with me. Who gains anything with these guys buying and selling land, except the guys buying and selling land? The rest of us pay more rent, more on the mortgage... Well, I ain't got a mortgage, and I will be paying rent when he finally gives me the push.' He laughed, swelling out his cheeks. 'I just don't play things right round here. You see me and Nadine get on. And that is not the smartest thing, not in this house. The property developer, he don't like that one bit, not now he's done with his missus.'

'I can see why you and Ace are not best friends.'

'He won't even give me a key. Can you believe it? I am a grown man. I've been here four months and I have to ring the doorbell to come and go. How you think that makes me feel?'

'A little unwelcome. How do you get on with Nick?'

'Better. Me and big brother are OK. He's a capitalist too, but he's not very good at it.' Mo was suddenly coughing. A bit of toast had caught in his throat. He spluttered, took a swig of coffee. 'See? Telling family secrets. That's what it does for you.'

Jack rose. He held out his hand.

'Nice to meet you, Mo.'

They shook hands once more. A way of parting. Jack had taken a liking to Mo. Wouldn't lend him money though. Even if he had any.

'Got to work for a living.'

'Yup, dance for the organ grinder.'

Jack gathered up his bits and pieces and went into the kitchen. And for a minute or so, he considered the point of working for a living. Sometimes it was plain stupid, useless, a waste of materials. Maybe this job was. An island when a table would do fine. Bricks when slips would work better.

But the monkey can't question the grinder if he wants to get fed.

Dance for the guy who turns the handle.

Over the next half hour, he located the joists. It was simple enough from the nail heads in the floorboards. He laid out parallel lines of masking tape across the outline of the island, to reveal the position of the underlying joists.

The body of the island rested on four of them. The problem was neither end was on a joist. Jack would need to move the island along five inches and then one end would be on a joist, but not the other. For both ends to rest on a joist, the island would have to be a little longer. Or shorter.

A nice conundrum. He looked over his parallel lines, very neat, but he certainly couldn't begin work until he had agreed with Ace both the position and size of the island.

Jack phoned and spoke to a secretary who told him Ace was in a meeting for the next hour. Jack sent a text, expressing the problem as clearly as he could in the text space allowed. Now he had an hour to wait till his client was free to reply. What to do in the time? Go down to Nadine. No, no, this house was too crowded. He could bring some bricks out to the patio. Or he could bank the money Ace had given him.

But was surprised to get a response, which made him suspect 'in a meeting' was the standard reply.

Do nothing, Jack, until we discuss this. I shall be back by 9.30 this evening.

What? Did Ace expect him to come back this evening? He had a date. This wasn't on. No way.

He texted back: *Can't make it. I have an important appointment this evening.*

He had a life, other than building work, thank you very much. Just because Ace hadn't thought this through, he couldn't expect Jack to come back in the evening. He had a date. How many of those did he have?

He wondered how it would fit with Nadine. The date. Hell, it was only a pizza date. Might be nothing. Or something. And he and Nadine could be nothing at all. No rings were exchanged.

When the reply came, it wasn't a complete surprise.

Be there, if you want the job.

He did. No argument. His mortgage depended on it. Ace knew that well enough. Knew the only money Jack had was what he was paying him. So the date with Penny was out. Goodbye, Penny.

Unless he could get away in time. He and Penny were due to meet at 7.30 pm. This was only a sussing out date. One of those where you are sizing each other up, scoring points for appearance and shared interests, deducting where you conflicted. Sometimes you wanted to leave in five minutes. And just stayed out of politeness.

If he told Penny that he had to leave by 9, there would still be plenty of time to eat their pizzas and fill in the score card. Yes, he'd stick with it.

Odds on it'd be no deal anyway.

Jack went downstairs to tell Nadine he was leaving till the evening. At least that was his excuse for seeing her again. She was in her studio, which he'd barely noted before, having seen little but her. Clearly the room had been a kitchen, with the sink and draining board still present. There were a lot of pictures on the walls, a few in frames, but most tacked up in temporary fashion. She was seated, drawing in pastels at a table. The image was bright and colourful, a woman coming out of a tangle of jungle vegetation.

'This time I'll look at your pictures,' he said.

'Is that why you're here?' She was sketching in some foliage.

'I can't do any more today,' he said. 'Till I see Ace.'

'Why's that?'

Jack explained how the island needed to be either shorter or longer. And how Ace had ordered him back this evening.

Nadine laughed. A little cruelly, he thought.

'You're learning fast,' she said, 'My husband has to call the shots. I'm sorry I can't help. But you know what I think of his crazy island.'

Jack did, and saw no point discussing it.

'Did you meet Mo?' she said.

'He says he's your mate.'

'We get on. But I wouldn't marry him.' She chuckled. 'One Baldwin has been way more than enough.'

'Well, I'm stuck with Ace,' said Jack. 'Nick screwed me over. But Ace is the boss this time round. I've got to play ball. I'll be back this evening. And oh yes, the house side door to the garden is still open...'

She rose. They embraced.

'We have to think what to tell Ace,' she said. Jack screwed his eyes, puzzled. 'Jack the spy's report. The one we didn't discuss when you were last here.'

He understood. Ace would want details.

'You'll have to have another lover,' he said.

'How do you know I haven't?'

'Have you?'

'That's for you to find out. You'll have to watch me.'

'I'll do that.'

'Thank you, but before you go,' she said, 'I'd like your advice. Builder's eye. Across the road at the Community Garden. I'm the co-ordinator for it. Part time. Just a few minutes. Will you come? I'll be very grateful.'

'I've nothing better to do.'

Chapter 6

They crossed the road to the community garden. Around it was a bright coloured hoarding, about eight feet high. The artwork consisted of cartoon type birds and insects, and vegetation in jolly hues. Why did it make Jack feel uncomfortable? Well, it was a garden for a kick off and he didn't know one end of a plant from the other. And such places were always full of people who did. When he was married to Alison, she would drag him along to National Trust houses full of pictures, and gardens with plants that had Latin names. They made him feel ignorant. It was like being in libraries, only worse. In a library, he could always go to the astronomy section, or the quick pick. Or even go to the fiction shelves, at least they were alphabetical, and he could find the few authors he knew. But a garden? G for grass, T for tree, F for flower. Then what?

He would never, not in a hundred years, have gone into this place on his own. To do what, for heaven's sake? But now he was accompanying Nadine who had a bunch of keys.

'We don't use the front gate when the garden isn't open to the public,' she explained as they walked round the hoarding with its giant ladybirds, spiders and ants. 'It's heavy, with three locks. But there's a side gate.'

They turned the corner, down a side street. Jack's phone rang. He glanced at the screen. It was from his daughter.

'Better take this,' he said to Nadine. 'My daughter. Might be important.'

Nadine was opening the padlock on the small side gate.

'Hello, Mia,' he said. 'What's up?'

'Mum's in hospital.'

'What's happened?'

'She was in a car accident,' said Mia. 'I don't know the details. But she's got broken bones in her leg and shoulder. And she's having an operation. She's not dead or anything, but is going to be in hospital for a few days. So I'm staying with you.'

That sounded like an order. Which of course it was. He was second in charge, but with first in charge out of action, he had a temporary promotion. And no further say in the matter.

'How did you find out?'

'She phoned the school from the hospital. I was called out of class. I had to go to the secretary's office where I spoke to Mum on the phone. She said I had to call you, and say I had to stay at your place for the time being. So there were are. I've done what I was told.'

What was there to say? Mum in hospital. He was in charge.

'I'll see you after school,' he said. 'We'll have to do some shopping. There's nothing in the house.' Thank heavens he had money.

'We can visit Mum in hospital this evening.'

'Yeh, we can. Buy her some flowers. I'll text her that you're staying with me. See you later, we can catch up then.'

'I was called out of Spanish,' said his daughter. 'Hasta la vista.'

She ended the call. So that was his evening organised. And there was the matter of Penny. That was settled too. Date cancelled. He'd tell her the truth. That would make a change. And reschedule.

Nadine had gone into the garden. She'd left the door ajar. He peered in nervously.

'There are no dragons,' she called.

There were plants everywhere. To be expected. Some in raised beds made with thick, heavy timbers. Quite a good job, their construction. The ground was covered in wood chippings. Nadine was right. There were no dragons. He wandered timidly. That bed had sunflowers, probably sunflowers, though he wouldn't bet on it. And roses, he could be sure of them, big with lots of petals, and prickles on the stems. There was a pond with built up wooden sides, the water low. It was a brown green colour with a couple of white flowers floating on the surface amid flat floating leaves. At the centre of the garden was a long shipping container, painted in green and browns, presumably full of tools and whatever else they needed here.

'The garden isn't open today?' he enquired.

'We open three days a week: Thursday, Friday, Saturday. We'd like to open more days but we're short of volunteers. The rule is two garden hosts for each session. Just in case there's trouble.'

'So we have it to ourselves today,' he said. He looked about him, at the raised beds, at the shipping container. Unsure what he should be seeing, not an unknown feeling in his garden visits.

'What's the problem?' he said.

'We've no running water,' said Nadine. 'And there's been no rain for well over a month. We've got rain barrels, lots of them, and they're all empty. People bring water in, but it's a dribble. We need a lot of it, and I mean a lot. Or this garden is going to be dead in a week or two.'

'Can't you carry it over from your place, buckets and watering cans, in a wheelbarrow?'

'Did it. Once. Then Ace stopped it. I thought OK, I'll do it when he's out and keep shtum. But his mother spilled the beans, and Ace said if I do it again, he'd lock me out of my studio.' She shrugged. 'As you know, it's his house. He can do that. So that source is verboten.'

'You really don't get on.'

'It's a dead marriage,' she said.

Jack looked around. It was dry alright. Even he could tell that. Once he'd been told.

'I'm not a dowser,' he said.

'Well, there's always mains water...' She hesitated, then added, 'I wondered if...'

'You'd have to get the water board to connect you.'

Nadine shook her head. 'They want three thousand quid. Which we haven't got.'

Jack whistled at the sum. And knew immediately what she was about to suggest.

'You thinking of an illegal connection?'

'Let's say unofficial.' She smiled broadly. 'Let me show you.'

He followed her, out through the gate and onto the pavement.

'There,' she said. She was pointing to a black, metal plate in the pavement about the size of a small food plate. It had the word 'Water' moulded into it and was about a foot from the hoarding. 'Must have been for the water to the house before it was demolished 15 years ago. Could that be piped into the garden?'

'Maybe,' mused Jack. 'Depends whether the water is still connected. They might have cut it off in the middle of the road. In which case, that accounts for the 3000 quid they want. To dig up the road and reconnect. But it's possible it might still be flowing to here. I'd need to have a look, and if it's flowing, think what's best to do.' He looked again at the small metal plate and ran a finger round the perimeter. 'I need a few tools. I'll bring some over. And I'll need a hose if you have one.'

'There's one in the container,' she said.

Jack left her and went to his van which was over the road by the house.

Nadine went back into the community garden through the side gate, which she left open for Jack. She could hardly bear to look about her. Plants dying, the pond had never been so low. Who knows how long this drought could go on for? But it was possible they could get water 'unofficially'.

Worth a go. Though if they were caught, she'd be in the line of fire.

She went to the shipping container. The double doors at the front had two padlocks. Nadine unlocked them and swung one of the doors wide. The container was about eight yards long and three wide. There was no light inside, only that which spilled in through the double doors. On the left were rows of tools: spades, forks, hoes, sledgehammers, rakes, brooms, trowels and so forth. Further in were metal shelves, and it was from one of these that she brought down a length of garden hose. It had never been used as they had no piped water. Just been taking up space in the hope that it might be useful one day. They had too much of that sort of stuff. The container needed a good clear out. Things just got thrown in and then buried.

Tomorrow.

Her phone rang. It was Sally.

'Hello, Sally,' she said. 'What are you ringing about?'

'I'm here.'

Nadine stepped out of the container with the coiled hose. There was Sally at the gate, her school bag on her back. Nadine dropped the hose and went to her. She could tell by her daughter's face something was wrong.

'What are you doing out of school?'

Sally handed her mother a screwed up piece of paper. Nadine unscrewed it, there was the school crest at the top with the Latin motto, *Fideliter*. The letter was from the Principal and was addressed to Mr Baldwin. And dated a week ago. With some trepidation, she began reading. A little unsure about what it was saying, she began again from the top. His prose style was somewhat formal, but clear enough by the end.

'This is addressed to your father,' she said. 'And it says you've been expelled. Is that true?'

'Yes.' Sally was looking very scared, very young.

'It says you were dealing drugs. Can that be true?'

She nodded. 'I bought them from Mo.'

What on earth had that piece of pig's tripe got her daughter into? Nadine had bankrolled him, made him breakfast time and again, defended him against Ace. That was history.

She'd chop his balls off.

Working to keep her temper, she said, 'This letter is a week old. What have you been doing all this time?'

Sally started crying. Nadine took her by the hand. 'Tell me the full story. There are worse things on Heaven and Earth. Let's sit down.'

She led her daughter to a metal bench under a rose arch. They sat side by side. Half of her wanted to be angry, very angry, the sensible side saw this wasn't the occasion for a telling-off.

'So what have you been doing for the last week?' she said.

'Dad drives me in. I head for the back gate. He drives off pretty quick. You know Dad, doesn't stick around. I go off to the station and take a train up west. I've been going into shops, to museums, and coming home when I'm expected.'

'You were scared to tell us?'

Sally nodded and sniffed, wiped her eyes with the back of her hand. 'It's not all.'

'Get it all out. I can't help you if I don't know what for.'

Sally was suddenly weeping helplessly. 'I am so sorry, Mum...' Her shoulders shook, her face had crumpled like a collapsed pie.

The state of her. Nadine suddenly knew.

'Are you pregnant?'

Her daughter nodded without looking at her mother.

'Don't tell me it's Mo.'

'It's not Mo. One of his friends. I've been bunking off. For a few months. Mo took me to this house in Plaistow where his friends were smoking weed, taking coke, all sorts. I met this guy...'

'One of Mo's mates?'

'Yes.'

'Are you still seeing this friend of Mo's?'

She shook her head. 'I haven't seen him for weeks.'

Nadine took this in. Expelled, pregnant. She could almost laugh. Ace had not wanted to send her to the local school because of the 'bad behaviour'. And now here she was at her posh, expensive school, pregnant and dealing dope. There was no point giving her a lecture. Not now. She was as miserable as sin. The worst had happened. The last thing she needed was a severe lecture. Maybe a talk on contraception, but not now.

'How pregnant are you?'

'About three months, I think.'

'Have you been sick?'

She nodded. 'In the mornings. I've managed to hide it. Dad never notices anything, and you don't come upstairs till I'm off to school. Well, not really school.' She began weeping, her head sinking into her hands.

'I get it, sweetheart,' said Nadine putting an arm round her daughter's shoulders. 'I'm fully briefed, as they say on the cop shows. The expulsion is done and dusted. Too late to do anything about that. You are out, your school days done. As for the pregnancy, there's two options. And I am sure you know what they are.'

Sally nodded. 'Keep it, or have an abortion.'

'Well, love, what do you want to do?'

Chapter 7

Jack levered up the circular plate with a cold chisel and hammer. Nadine and Sally were in the garden, heads lowered, talking fervently. Something was up, he could tell from the girl's evident distress, but he had no idea what.

Health related? Could be a school thing. Bullying, something like that.

The plate out, he looked into the hole. About six inches down was a stopped pipe. All he had to do was unscrew the end. Water would either flow or it had been capped in the road. If the latter, the garden would stay dry. Jack didn't have a road drill.

With a wrench and hammer, he loosened the end. Water began dribbling out as it eased. So it was still connected. He tightened it again and went into the garden and collected the hose. Nadine and Sally were still talking on the bench under the bower. Nadine gave him the briefest of waves, mouthing 'sorry, Jack' as he passed.

He came out into the street with the coil of hose. Over the next five minutes, getting wet as the water gushed free as he attempted direct it, Jack connected the hose pipe with a couple of jubilee clips to the street connection. There was leakage, but little he could do about that without the proper fitting.

Jack took the gushing hose into the garden. He gave a thumbs up to Nadine.

'We've got water!'

'Well done, Jack,' she called back.

He took the hose to the nearest barrel and began filling it. Pleased that he'd got something done today, even if he wasn't being paid for it. But this was the boring bit. Just holding the hose, as someone had to stay with it, or the pressure of water would force the hose out of the barrel. Just as well, he wasn't working on the kitchen island. Though, he did need to get to the bank to pay the money in. He'd get Nadine to take over.

With the barrel about half full, Nadine came over with Sally whose face was streaked with dried tears.

'I've got to take Sally to the clinic. Sorry, Jack. Family emergency. Can you fill the barrels for me? Please.' Her eyes large, holding the hand of her distressed daughter.

How could he refuse?

'Sure,' he said. 'You go.'

'Thank you so much, Jack. Here's the keys. Lock the container and gate when you go.' She handed him the bunch of keys. 'I'm sorry to leave you like this, and I wouldn't if it wasn't an emergency.'

'Go,' he said. 'I can manage a hose.'

She kissed him on the cheek. They would have embraced but he was directing the hose into the barrel and they had no wish to telegraph their relationship to Sally. Whatever it was. Or wasn't.

Mother and daughter left him.

Over the next hour, Jack went from barrel to barrel. Some of the barrels he had to bring closer as the hose wasn't long enough. He got a soaking every so often, as he couldn't turn the water off, but it was summer, and water did you no harm.

It was odd being in a garden by himself. In charge. With the keys, for heaven's sake. But his ignorance didn't matter, he was simply an appendage to the hose. The servant who had to hold the end in the barrels and let then fill up. The pressure was fierce, like an alive thing, the hose struggled to be free, but Jack pushed the hose well inside as the water poured in.

There was a point, and he couldn't have said exactly when, that he began to go hazy. Then groggy, becoming quite stupid with it. Wet through, he collapsed.

When he opened his eyes again, he knew he'd been unconscious a while. Minutes, half an hour? He couldn't say. Jack was lying in a puddle, the hose gushing free. He had just enough sense to realise what had happened to him. He'd had a diabetic coma, a short one he reckoned, but he couldn't know for sure. His doctor had warned him this might happen if he didn't eat properly. Well, he hadn't eaten since breakfast, and then only toast. And his body was crying out for food. Diabetes, his body insulin awry and all that involved. Eat little and often, the doctor had said. Lots of fruit and veg.

Wise words, unheeded.

Jack scrambled to his feet and staggered a few steps. He was giddy, he was soaked, but with just enough sense to know he had to eat. Somehow, he made his way to the gate. Out into the street, and then along the hoarding, supporting himself on it with one arm.

Food. That was his one thought. Eat.

Chapter 8

Jack ate at the Forest Cafe. Fortunately, they knew him, and he'd with mumbled words and signs managed to get it across that he wasn't drunk, but was diabetic. They weren't totally convinced but fed him anyway. He'd begun with fruit juice and biscuits. And then slowly consumed an all day breakfast, oozing back to full consciousness as the nourishment coursed through his bloodstream, enlivening his body and brain.

Bringing him back to the sentient world.

He rose and thanked the cafe workers, feeling almost OK. Certainly well enough to get back and sort things out back in the garden. He'd simply stumbled out, must've left the gate open and the container-shed.

The Forest Cafe accepted he hadn't been drunk.

'Eat properly,' called Joe from behind the counter as Jack left. 'I had an uncle who died on a bus.'

'Good advice,' he said as he stepped into the street.

Good advice indeed. He must keep some emergency rations with him. Biscuits. Or maybe something he didn't like very much so he wouldn't be tempted to eat it all before it was needed.

He strode rapidly, pleased to be once again in the land of the living. His damp clothes were drying, reminding him of when he was a kid, swimming in his underclothes, and putting outer clothes back on. His body would dry them. He'd be a little shrivelled, but no harm done.

How had he left the garden? The state he'd been in earlier, he could barely remember what he'd done. He definitely had not closed the gate when he'd staggered out. He had been filling the water barrels... The hose! It had been like a writhing snake. How long had he been in the cafe? It would be pouring free, drenching heaven knows what. The garden gate wide open.

And illegal water flooding.

Jack turned down the side road to get to the side gate, and at once saw the water board van. The hose was lying on the pavement, detached from the water point. Jack knew he hadn't done it, he hadn't been capable of anything so organised. And there was the engineer coming out of the garden, scratching his head. No doubt looking for someone to blame. He was in brown overalls, with curly hair, thinning at the front, and clutching a laptop.

Jack turned about and crossed the road to his van. He opened up and got in the front. From his seat, he could see down the side road, and watched surreptitiously, pretending to be going through some papers. The man wouldn't stay long, he was sure.

The water board man kept looking in the gate, as if someone was hiding, which they were, but not where he was looking. The man looked up and down the road, in the garden again, and after a few minutes, obviously fed up with waiting, got in the van and drove off.

Jack came out now that the road was clear. He must lock up and skedaddle. There would be hell to pay on this. Worry about that later. Jack dragged the hose into the garden. Someone else could coil it up. He locked the container, having some trouble with the locks and keys, but worked the right ones out by trial and error.

He was on the way to the side gate, when the man came in.

'I thought someone had to be here,' he said with a thin smile. 'I came in earlier, water gushing everywhere. Hose connected illegally to the outside point. But no one here. That container open. Like the Mary Celeste.'

'I don't know Mary Celeste,' said Jack, intentionally misunderstanding. 'You've got the wrong address.'

The man looked at him quizzically. 'No, no. The hose was connected to the outside water point. Illegally. You've been stealing water.'

'Not me,' said Jack. 'I just came in to lock up.'

'And who are you?'

Who was he, indeed. Somebody, but who?

'Nick.'

'And are you in charge?'

'Yes, I am.' And indeed he was. It couldn't be said to be a lie. He had the keys. Who else was there?

'Do you know stealing water from the water board is punishable by a fine of up to one thousand pounds?'

Jack blew out his cheeks at the figure.

'I haven't got it with me,' he said. 'Can you come back later?'

'I am here now, Nick. And this is serious, mate. It's obvious water has been stolen. I've seen all the full water barrels, and the hosepipe connected to our supply. Unauthorised. Which is theft in plain English.' He opened his laptop. 'What's your surname, Nick?'

'Baldwin.'

'Nick Baldwin.' The man wrote it carefully. 'Got that. Address, Mr Baldwin?'

He gave Nick Baldwin's address. He knew it well enough from all the invoices he'd sent Nick. All unpaid.

'You will be fined for this, you know,' said the man. 'Stealing water is a criminal offence. And I must tell you, it is not company policy to let people off. It sets a bad example.'

'Can you really steal water?' said Jack. 'Adam's ale. It comes from the sea, and rains down on us. No one can own it.'

The man looked at him, unsure whether he was joking or not. 'This some sort of hippy place?' he finally said gesturing around at the plants and raised beds.

'Yes. A hippy place. We share this garden with the community.'

The man shook his head. 'Well, we are not hippies, Nick. We don't share. That water belongs to us. You want some, you pay for it. Or you pay a fine.'

And with that the man turned and left. Jack gave him a minute or two, and then went out himself. He locked the gate of the community garden. Someone was going to get fined. But it wouldn't be Nick as Nick didn't have a penny. And Jack would, hopefully, be long gone by the time they'd done their paperwork.

Chapter 9

Jack walked to the bank in Stratford. He had plenty of time as he couldn't work on the kitchen island until he'd sorted things out with Ace. Besides which, there wasn't much petrol in his van and he didn't want to spend money filling it up. Every penny had to be turned over twice before it left his hand. The mortgage came first, but he had to keep some back for food. He hoped further payment from Ace would be due, in spite of him doing next to nothing today. And oh yes, he'd have to give some money to Mia for lunches now that she'd be staying. Money didn't stick around long.

Food, food, once he had a roof over his head, it was number two. His diet was dreadful, and the doctor had warned him, he couldn't live on fry ups. Fruit and veg, cut down the carbs and he'd be fine.

Except he didn't like fruit and veg. Then again, collapsing wasn't a good alternative. He'd better start liking greens. That blackout, on his own in the garden, was a warning. Pathetic and predictable. It had resulted in a thousand pound fine for the garden, as he was pretty sure the water board would find out that Nick Baldwin had no connection with the place, and so they'd finally send the bill in to the right person. Nadine or whoever controlled their money. The garden registered office would be online somewhere. You could find it in five minutes.

So what should he tell Nadine? Tell her the water board came; he couldn't avoid telling her that. But he didn't have to say that he'd passed out. Just say the man came. It was bad luck.

Though it wasn't. Carelessness, bad diet. It was quite likely, if he hadn't blacked out, he could have detached the hose before the man came, and so no fine. His dumb coma had cost the garden a thousand quid. Though Nadine knew she was taking a risk. But she didn't know she was doing it with a diabetic builder. She lacked the full facts. How much did she need to know?

Likely their relationship would be a short one. Certainly would be if this got out.

Then again, she'd gone off with her daughter and left him in the garden with the keys. She had no right doing that. He wasn't in charge, no matter what she said. She was the boss in the garden. Which didn't stop him feeling responsible. The community garden couldn't have much money. These projects all worked on a shoestring. Surely, they could do a deal with the water board? Not from the sound of the man with the laptop. The poor suffering shareholders had to be recompensed.

It would take time before they sent in their demand. The water board would first contact Nick Baldwin, and he'd just pass the bill onto the receiver. The receiver would tell them that it wasn't applicable, Nick wasn't the man. And the bureaucratic wheels would grind on. Getting there in the end, to keep the shareholders out of the poorhouse.

At the bank, Jack paid all but £30 into his account. One gaping maw satisfied, he hoped. He walked home. On the way, he popped into a supermarket. Well aware of what food to buy after his episode earlier. A bunch of bananas and a bag of apples went into his basket. He considered a loaf of bread, but he ate too much bread, carbohydrate converted to sugar by his stomach, as Mia had informed him. He knew some, had read it up more and Mia filled in his gaps. And then he just ignored it, as if reading was sufficient remedy. Not this time, not ever. He didn't want to die on a bus like Joe's uncle.

Standing by the vegetable aisle, he contemplated what to buy. Not broccoli, tasteless stuff, or leeks, no good on their own. He needed something you could eat if you can't cook. He bought fresh peas, and some French beans; they just needed boiling. Lettuce was for rabbits, cucumber was all water. He completed his purchases with a can of tomatoes, some onions and pasta. Mia had taught him that with pasta and a can of tomatoes, with a little pepper, you can add just about any veg, and you have a meal. Which was almost edible.

At home, he went online and sent an email to Penny.

Sorry, Penny, family emergency. My daughter's mother has gone into hospital after a car accident, and so I have to look after my 15 year old daughter for the next few days. Sorry to be a pain, I'll reschedule when her mother is out of hospital.

It was a bit formal, and had 'sorry' twice. He could say how much he'd like to meet her, but that was only half true now that Nadine was in the picture. But Nadine was his boss's wife, and he was being paid to keep an eye on her. Anything could go wrong, and already had with the water problem and a big fine in the offing. Sure to add to his popularity. So like the typical male of the species, he figured best keep another iron in the fire.

Jack batted the wording back and forth, changing a phrase, putting it back, and decided that he would keep the text as it was. Stick with the truth. Always wise, except when dealing with the water board.

*

Nadine and Sally were in a pizza house, sharing a large vegetarian pizza. Sally wasn't vegetarian but Nadine was, mostly. It annoyed Ace who thought such peccadillos unnatural, and that kept her to it.

They had been to the British Pregnancy Advisory Service where Sally had had an interview. Nadine had sat in the waiting room, attempting to read a magazine but was too distracted. Her daughter was pregnant. She couldn't look at fashion pages or read her star sign.

The options were twofold: go full term or have an abortion. Having an abortion was final, providing Sally was OK with it. But going full term had all sorts of repercussions. The baby could be given up for adoption. That was unlikely, she reckoned, as there were herself, Sally of course, and Sally's granny to assist with parenting. But she had a divorce coming up, and oh Lord, where would she be living after that? Not downstairs from Ace until the child was grown up. Save her from that fate. She wanted to get away from him, clean out of his ken, be independent.

Babies don't allow freedom. They pen you, force you to put them first. Incredible how much power they have for something so tiny. Neglect was a crime, not that she would; a child was a child, and deserved to be properly brought up. But to be co-parenting with Ace's mother, with Ace there in the background, controlling her through his bank balance, was a horror film.

She had said none of this to Sally. Simply said it was her choice. Nadine sincerely believed that. It wasn't the role of the state or the church to interfere with women's bodies, but the choice of every woman whether to have a child or not. It was Sally's body, stupid girl, it would be her pregnancy to continue or cut short. Sally was not quite of adult age, but had only a year or so to go. And whatever she decided, Nadine would go along with.

Horror or not.

She hoped her daughter would opt for an abortion, simpler all round. Sally would then not be a teenage single parent but could get on with her life. Not that she'd be damned if she had a child, as mother and granny would be drawn in for childcare.

A grandchild did have its attractions. Babies and toddlers are awfully cute. Dependent, they hold your hand, they follow you. But post primary school, who knows what anxieties lay down the road? Nadine herself would be in Ace's sphere much longer than she'd hoped. After the divorce, she could see it, endless. They could be bringing up a child, still arguing as the child, boy or girl, went through its babyhood, infancy, childhood. On and on, to time immeasurable. Till she was wrinkled and grey.

Nadine was conflicted when it came to motherhood. What was the old adage? The enemy of art is the pram in the hall. Something like that. And sure, there were times she'd felt utterly confined, unable to do anything but soothe a child. There were other times when she'd been overcome with love. But she'd had Ace, the father, always in the wings, sometimes centre stage. His demands, his control. Sally's child had a father too. Whoever he was, however feckless. What rights did he have? Should he even be told?

Sally came out of the interview room. She said to her mother that the counsellor wanted to talk to both of them. So it was a threesome in the small room, around the table. The counsellor was a pleasant, plumpish, middle aged Asian woman. Very sensible, not dominating at all. Sally had decided, when taken through the options, to have an abortion.

It was now a question of where and when.

Chapter 10

When Mia came in from school, Jack noted her bag was light.

'No homework?'

'None.' She had slumped on the sofa. 'School finishes at the end of the week. It's all games and reading, and lectures from teachers telling us how important next year is going to be, with GCSEs and all that. And if we want a good job, or to get to university, bla bla bla.'

'It is important,' he said. Wishing, every so often, that he had listened to those lectures when he'd been her age.

She flapped a dismissive hand. 'I know, I know. If I've heard it once, I've heard it a hundred times.' She imitated an earnest teacher. 'Year 11, girls, is the beginning of the most important period of your lives. I cannot emphasise enough how important it is. Put your phone down at the back there.'

He smiled, in spite of himself.

'They said that to you, didn't they?' she said. 'Not the girls bit. The rest.'

'More or less. And I didn't take a blind bit of notice. Now look at me.'

'You do alright.'

'If I'd have worked, put my head down, instead of bunking off, I could be...' he thought of the possibilities. 'A professor of astrophysics.'

'Who is more useful to society?' she said languidly, 'a professor of astrophysics or a builder? Discuss.'

'I know who gets paid more,' he said.

'OK, I'll be a professor of astrophysics then. And send a rocket ship to explore Olympus Mons on Mars. Or I could go myself. What do you think of that?'

The idea pleased him. Mia was bright, and at 15 well on the way to being a young woman. Hormone charged, sure enough, but she still enjoyed coming out on the Flats with him and the telescope. The next few years were important, he knew, but she wouldn't take any speeches from him. Not with his school record. He'd leave that side exclusively to Alison, her mother, who was headteacher of a primary school. And lecturer in chief.

'You won't need a chit from me for a Mars trip,' he said.

'Bones degenerate in space,' she mused. 'A six to nine month journey there, with all that radiation, astronauts run the risk of sterility. Do you want grandchildren?' Before he could answer, she went on, 'The atmosphere on Mars is one hundredth of that on Earth. You have to live in a bubble, go out in a massive space suit. There are dust storms that blow at 200 miles per hour for months. If anything goes wrong, you are well and truly screwed.'

'Sounds like you're talking yourself out of it.'

'I'll get my degree in astrophysics,' she said ponderously, 'and then I'll decide whether to sign up. Or step back and let another guinea pig suffocate on Mars. What food we got?'

She rose, and went into the kitchen, leaving the door ajar.

'Bit sparse,' she said, opening and closing cupboard doors. 'Better than usual though. But needs topping up.' She came out. 'Let's go shopping.'

Jack had anticipated this reaction. His earlier shop was to take the heat off, make it look like he was eating well. But he agreed, it was a bit sparse. Though all he had was £21, and Mia needed lunch money.

'Just a few things,' he said.

Mia changed out of her school uniform, and into jeans and a t-shirt. She had some clothes here, but most were at her mother's.

They walked down the road together. There were plane trees on either side of the road, their full summer leaves curling in the drought. The sun was hot, the sky clear. A perfect night to go out on the Flats, but he had to go and see Ace at 9.30. Maybe afterwards, as he couldn't imagine it being a long chat.

It was agreed they would visit Alison in hospital after they'd eaten.

They passed his van and the house where he'd been working. Jack pointed it out and told her that he was building an island. That amused Mia.

'Bigger than Australia?'

'Twice the size.'

'How are you going to get it in the house?'

'Damn. Never thought of that. Maybe just the size of the Isle of Dogs.'

They passed the community garden with its colourful hoarding. He said nothing about that, or the thousand pound fine.

Chapter 11

Nick was in the sitting room, half watching *Bargain Hunt*. He was stretched out in an armchair, his stockinged feet on an ottoman. He had rolled up the sleeves of his blue shirt, the collar open wide, and undone his belt to take the pressure off his middle-aged spread.

His eyes were watery, he had been weeping. It simply came, anything brought it on. Even this stupid antiques show. He didn't know why he was watching it. Though what else could he do?

No one wanted him. Not kids, not wife.

The screen was 60 inch, the same size as the one the bailiffs took yesterday. The show was mid-auction: a middle aged man and woman were excited as the vase they bought for twenty pounds had reached the heady heights of sixty and was still rising. They couldn't believe it. Seventy pounds now. The woman punched the man on the shoulder. 'I told you,' she mouthed. The auctioneer was holding his gavel up. He wanted a bid at eighty. And he got it. The woman raised both arms in triumph...

Marta, his mother, strode into the room and turned off the TV.

'I was watching that,' he said.

'Afternoon TV will be the death of you.'

'I'm dead already,' he said with a long sigh. 'What is the point? I don't know what to do with myself. How to live any more.'

She had taken a hard back chair and sat by him. He was watching the screen as if the auction might magically re-appear.

'I have been thinking,' said Marta, 'this is not the best place for you. Not with Ace here.'

'That dung beetle. I should have used a carving knife, not my bare hands.'

'It's no good talking that way.'

'I only needed a few more days,' he went on, as if she had not spoken. 'Money was due today. I bet it has come. Fat lot of good it'll do anyone. I've got nothing. Less than nothing. All that remains of me is a smell.'

'Things are bad,' she said, patting his hand. 'That cannot be denied. But you can't simply blame your brother.'

'Why not?'

'You were overstretched, taking big risks. I'm not a finance person, but even I could tell you were getting into deep water.'

'And so I drowned, while brother Noah saves all the family in his ark.'

'You are in his ark too,' said Marta firmly.

'I don't want to be. Believe me. But I haven't got a life-boat.' He sighed and looked to the ceiling. 'I want to go home, but I can't. Not on my own to that empty house. I'd slash my wrists in the bath.'

'Don't talk that way. I forbid it.'

'I've tried six times to talk to Anne, she won't speak to me. I've sent texts, I've emailed. She's in another dimension where I don't exist.'

'Some things can't be rushed,' she said. 'She has lost so much too, and must decide whether she wants to be with you and build your lives again.'

'And if she doesn't?'

'Then so be it. It's the Lord's way.'

'I don't like your Lord. He doesn't like me.'

'I'm sure that's part of the problem,' she said adamantly.

'She has the children.'

'That's another matter. Anne cannot deny you access. You have been a good father. You don't beat her. And how long will she want to stay with her mother?'

'Not long.' He half grinned, then shut it down as inappropriate to his misery. 'A week is all she can take.'

'You see? Be patient. It's nearly the end of term. She has taken the children out of school for the last week. But will she want them to start a new school in September?'

'No,' he said thoughtfully, biting a knuckle. 'Ben and Liz like their school.'

'So she has problems too. You must stop phoning her. In fact, give me your phone.'

The phone was on the arm of his chair. He shouldn't let his mother baby him, but he couldn't summon the strength to argue. Marta took it. He shrugged. What did it matter? It was pointless phoning someone who didn't reply. That was obvious, but he couldn't stop himself.

'What am I going to do?' he said. 'I have all this useless time. It doesn't stop. I want to sleep for a century.'

'I've had an idea,' she said. 'It's no good sitting here brooding, watching daytime TV. That's for old age pensioners. Not for my sons. You need to get up. Move. I thought we could go away for a few days. Get you out of Ace's house.'

'Go where?'

He couldn't imagine anywhere else being different. He would still be broke. He would still be himself. Without his family.

'Broadstairs,' she said. 'You always liked that.'

'I did,' he said. 'I went there with Anne and the kids two years ago.'

'We used to go when you were children. Remember? You, me, Ace and Mo.'

'Yes. I liked the sandy beach and the chalk cliffs. A seagull stole a bun from Ben...' he laughed. 'You should have seen his face. The gull squawking and wheeling in the air, and he was running about trying to get it back.' He smiled at the memory, just a couple of years back when all was going well. 'I like the sea. I would watch it, the waves breaking in the surf. Like a tune that goes on forever. All that green water, rolling in from the horizon, the dome of sky above our heads. It makes me think of eternity, how insignificant we are. What a lot of fuss we make.' He turned to his mother. 'I could manage time there. When shall we go?'

'Tomorrow,' she said. 'We'll catch a train. I've already found a bed and breakfast. My treat. We are going to the seaside.'

Chapter 12

Nadine was drumming her fingers on the table. She was in her studio, on the phone. She didn't like the picture she'd done that morning, lying on the table before her. Too derivative.

'Tell him it's a family emergency, Petra,' she said. 'I know all about Ace's meetings.'

'I'll try.'

Nadine put the phone on speakerphone and laid it on the table. So much had happened since she'd done that picture. It was colourful, sort of impressionist, the woman coming out of foliage, but it lacked any emotion. The woman needed to be tearful, as if her world is falling to pieces, or it's just a woman coming out of foliage.

'What do you want, Nadine?' said Ace sharply.

'We have a family emergency,' she said. 'Your daughter.'

He sighed. 'What has she done now?'

'She's been expelled. Let me read you this letter...' She began reading, 'Dear Mr Baldwin...'

'How dare you open letters addressed to me!'

'I did not open it,' she yelled. 'Your daughter has had it for a week. She opened it. Why do you never listen to me?'

'I listen, oh I listen, Ms Wise Woman. It's all I ever do. But have you even once taken any notice of a thing I've said?'

'That isn't a question,' she said wearily. 'And this is hardly a conversation. Not between adults. In brief, Mr Bigshot: your daughter has been expelled for dealing drugs.

And she's pregnant. If you want to hear more I suggest you come home.'

Nadine closed the call before he could reply. She was in a fury. How he exasperated her! Straight away accusing her of opening his letters. He had certainly opened hers. But she'd told him this time, firing both barrels. She drummed her fingers on the table. Dreadful picture, the quiescent woman. How long before he phones back? Give it half a minute...

Her phone rang. And rang. Should she answer or let him stew?

She picked it up, and said, 'I am not going to have a row over the phone.'

'Is it true what you just told me?'

'Yes.'

'Sally has been expelled and she is pregnant?'

'Yes.'

'You spoil her, Nadine, you give in to her. I knew this would happen.'

'Mystic Meg predicts all.' She laughed without any mirth. 'Then you've no need to hear what we're going to do about it.'

She closed the call and turned off her phone. Let him fume. She tore up the picture. No feeling in it. Just colour. He'll be here. Give him half an hour. He'll be storming in accusing her of witchcraft. What to do in the meantime? There was a grant application she needed to get in. But no way could she concentrate on a children's garden workshop and pond dipping. Her head wasn't her own. Ace was striding about her stage berating her. She was yelling back. Two players circling each other. She was the audience too, the scene shifters and lighting crew.

A play without an ending, a middle, with constant beginnings. There had to be a murder or there'd never be a final act.

Nadine left her room. She went up the stairs and through the kitchen. Marta was making tea. The two women did not speak, and made no eye contact. Nadine went out on to the patio. She would water the vegetables. That required little decision and less thought.

Chapter 13

'How did it happen?' said Jack.

Alison was sitting up in bed. She was in a ward with five other women, two sets of three beds on either side of a wide gangway. Jack was on a chair by her bed, Mia had gone off to find a vase for the flowers. Another fiver gone on those. Mia had brought her mother a book, *Catcher in the Rye*. It had been one of her course books that year. She had had more than enough of Holden Caulfield.

'I'll tell you when Mia's back,' said Alison. 'Don't want to say it twice.'

Jack felt like a class of kids, but said nothing. Alison was in hospital and it was his brief to be nice. A row on the ward wouldn't help either of them. Flowers and sympathy, that was his brief.

She had her right arm in plaster and a sling. Her chestnut hair was tied back in a ponytail. She had no make-up on, and was wearing a graceless hospital gown. Mia had the same hair, was similar height and build but Alison's body was more lived in, sterner, more sure of herself. Still good looking, but slipping into middle age. As Jack was himself. Nobody stands still.

'What shall we talk about then?' said Jack.

'The weather?'

'Hot and dry. Now what?'

'I hate hospitals.' She shrugged and winced a little as it pained her arm. 'It's not their fault. The staff are fine. I waited ages in emergency, but I can't blame anyone for that except the government. It's just that I am bored soppy. I'm

used to doing things. And I am going to be here three days.'
She rolled her eyes. 'Lord God save us.'

Mia returned with a vase of flowers.

'Lovely,' said Alison. 'Put it on that side, love.'

She already had one vase of flowers. More luxurious
than Jack and Mia's. Tall flowers, lots of blooms clustered
together on spears. Jack had no idea what they were, or
what he and Mia had brought for that matter. It's what you
did for a hospital visit; bring flowers.

Mia had sat down on the other side of the bed from
Jack.

'What happened, Mum?'

'I was crossing a junction this morning, driving into
work. I had the right of way. And this car hit me on the
side. I had my seatbelt on, of course. It would have been a
lot worse otherwise. The door was banged in, I was
smothered in airbag and couldn't move. By the time I
could, my whole right side was aching like hell. I've busted
my arm.' She raised the encased arm. 'And my right leg is
broken in two places. They're going to put a plate in
tomorrow. I've been x-rayed, and been seen by two
doctors. I do wish the food was better. Not even up to
school lunch standard.'

'What happened to the other driver?'

'Oh, he's fine. Got a smashed up car though. And he
can't get out of taking responsibility. A cop got his details
for me. My car has been towed away. But I'll be getting
another while it's repaired. And I'm stuck here while I'm
repaired.' She turned to her daughter. 'So you're going to
be with your dad for a few days.'

'I'll survive,' said Mia. 'But I need some clothes.'

'We'll drive over and collect some later,' said Jack.

'There's food in the fridge, you can have that too,' said
Alison. 'I know the junk you eat, Jack. No matter what you
tell me. I have seen with my own eyes. Take some fruit too.'

'We've been shopping,' said Mia.

'There's no point my food going to waste. How are you for money, Jack?'

'Fine,' he said awkwardly. He hated taking money from her. 'Just got paid.'

'You sure?'

'Yes.'

There was a brief silence. Jack wanted to leave. Hospital visits were boring, but you couldn't just arrive and go. This money stuff was belittling. Yes, she earned a lot more than he did. She was a head teacher, steady job, good income, but did she have to keep reminding him?

'Can you fill my water glass, Mia? There's a good girl.'

Mia filled the glass from a jug.

'Have you read *Catcher in the Rye*, Mum?' she said.

'Yes,' said Alison. 'At school. When I was your age. This pain of a boy knows everything about everything.'

'That's exactly what I thought,' said Mia. 'And ours is a girls' school. Why not have a book with a girl main character?'

'Good point. They had a choice, I'm sure,' said her mother. 'Bet you one of your teachers has done it before, knows it. It lessens her workload. That's the way it goes.' She picked up the book. 'I'll see if the book has improved after twenty years.'

Jack stood up.

'We've got to go,' he said. He reckoned this was about long enough. If he stayed longer he was sure they'd row about something. Besides which, as soon as he sat down by a hospital bed, any hospital bed, he wanted to leave. 'We've clothes to collect for Mia,' he added by way of excuse, 'and then I've got to see this client who is messing me about.'

'Come tomorrow evening,' said Alison. 'I'll have had my operation. Thank you for the flowers and the book. Don't forget to take the food in the fridge.'

They left her, tentatively opening the paperback as if it held bad memories.

Chapter 14

Nadine was watering the vegetables. She had the hose on spray and was getting a little wet, but she didn't care. It was only water and the day was warm. She'd come into the garden in the hope that she could stop arguing with Ace in her head. Sure she won, but so what? It left her pointlessly furious. He'd be here soon enough, save the words and energy. Ace was Sally's father, so there was no evading telling him what was going on. And he'd blame her, and she'd blame him. No need to rehearse it.

Water the tomatoes.

Roll on the divorce. Her solicitor had explained that she might have to wait two years. A Decree Nisi could only be granted for unreasonable behaviour, and whether Ace's behaviour was unreasonable was arguable. She was accusing him of bullying. Her solicitor had said a witness would be helpful. It had occurred to her, mid watering, that Nick would be a most willing one. He'd tried to throttle Ace, so surely would be willing to attest that Ace was a bully.

Nadine also suspected Ace was sleeping around, possibly call girls. Certainly their sex life had been dead for several years. For a while he'd kept trying with her, she'd put up with it from time to time, then he had stopped. Found another outlet, she suspected.

She needed to get hold of his mobile phone. Find out. Adultery was unreasonable behaviour. There'd be some-thing on his phone. Or just follow him. But that wouldn't work, he'd spot her too easily. But what about Jack? He could be a double agent. He was supposed to be watching her, but he was also in touch with her husband. Could at least talk to him, man to man. Get evidence for her.

Or here's a way out idea. She could be the adulterer. There was Jack conveniently in the wings. Likely he'd be a willing partner, though maybe not if he knew she'd be using it as grounds for divorce. He didn't have to be told. Nor did it mean necessarily their relationship couldn't continue. She could get things started, have to be at Jack's place, then wait till Jack had finished the wretched kitchen island and been paid. A week perhaps, that's all. Then admit her sin to Ace and his solicitor. It would make her the scarlet woman though. Not that her mother-in-law could think any worse of her. There was Sally to consider, but then Sally's behaviour had been so bad that whatever Nadine did could hardly match.

Even so, did she really want to look lustful in her daughter's eyes? Must she admit adultery? She needed to talk to her solicitor. Tomorrow. And somehow tell Jack she was willing. Notch up a few sessions. She was feeling so manipulative. Not simply an affair, but one to bring about a divorce. The best thing would be if Ace walked in on them. How could she engineer that?

Or get Jack watching Ace. The more options the better. She couldn't wait two years to get free of him.

Nadine had been watering the same spot for the last minute while she considered the repercussions of adultery and spying. There was a puddle around the peas. She directed the hose to a row of soft fruit.

'Nadine!'

She turned. There was Mo crossing the lawn. The brothers Baldwin! The only one of whom she didn't want to see in Hell was Nick. And that was only because she wanted him as a witness.

'Can you lend me a tenner, love?'

He was as scruffy as ever. Mo always looked as if he'd just got out of bed, hair awry, stubbly cheeks. He had on the same grubby t-shirt with the defiant black Olympians. A few hours earlier, he'd been a character, someone to tease Ace with. Now he was monstrous, a parasite and sponger, who had corrupted her daughter.

Mo had come through the hedge to the vegetable patch.

'You have the gall to ask me for a tenner!' she exclaimed.

'What do you mean?' he said, stopping, startled by her reaction.

'Where have you been all day?' she demanded.

'Out and about. With mates. You know.'

'Smoking weed?'

'Might've done. What is all this?'

His eyes were wide from weed smoking, his movement sluggish, half stoned motion. No longer charming. Uncaring. He had drawn her daughter into his dissolute life.

'Ace is right about you,' she said. 'You are a waste of space.'

Mo threw up his hands in disbelief.

'What have I done, Nadine?'

'Don't Nadine me. Stay away from me and my family. Or I'll give you the first wash you've had in a week.' She threatened him with the hose, turning the nozzle to a fierce stream.

'I don't get this. What's happened?'

'Sally has been expelled.'

'You're kidding. Expelled? Straight up, sis?'

'Stop that sister stuff. You can't claim me as part of your dope clan. Yes, expelled from school. You are her dealer, and not only that. You've been taking her around to your drug parties.'

'I wasn't forcing her. She wanted to come.'

'You are her uncle, Mo. More than twice her age. She's 17 and stupid. You're supposed to put her right, not get her pregnant.'

'She's pregnant?'

'Yes, pregnant. And my first thought was that it was you. But no, one of your scumbag mates, with uncle no doubt looking on.' She turned the hose in his direction. Mo jumped back. 'Ace is due soon. He's going to throw you onto the street. And three cheers, says I. When your mother finds out, you won't have a single defender in this house.'

'It's not the way you think...'

She turned the hose on him. He backed off, fighting the jet of water with flailing arms.

'You won't even listen, you cow.' Water was dripping down his face. 'You're just like Ace says, a feminist motor-mouth... I defended you.'

She stepped forward, directing the hose at him. Just catching him, as he backed further off.

'Scram, before Ace strangles you.'

'I'm not afraid of Ace. Or you, or anyone.' He was by the kitchen door. 'You're going to regret this, Nadine. I'll get you, you just wait, you self righteous bitch.'

And he was in the kitchen, and out of her sight. She wondered what his threats amounted to. She suspected it was bluster. Dopehead talk. She'd been taken in for too long, while he lied and sold weed to her daughter.

And what was worse, Ace had been right about him all the time.

Chapter 15

The three of them came down quietly to Nadine's sitting room. Neither Marta nor Nick knew what was going on with Sally, and so a clandestine meeting below stairs was agreed by her parents. Ace was reluctant, not comfortable in her space, but it was the only option for privacy.

Ace had taken the one armchair. Sally and Nadine were on the two-seater sofa. The room was small, quite cosy, with three of Nadine's paintings on the wall, bright colourful vegetation and cloudy skies, to alleviate the gloom of the basement.

Ace was in his grey suit, wearing his tie. Always the business man, even after a day's work. He didn't have casual wear as he said he had no casual time. His perennial joke was that holidays would be taken when he retired. Nadine doubted he ever would retire, or take holidays for that matter. Her husband was too restless, making money was his buzz. It had given him everything he had, and would give him more.

Nadine was determined to keep her temper. Well, for as long as possible, as he was bound to wind her up and she would break, surely. At least she'd begin quietly. Her hands were in her lap like a demure maiden aunt. Let someone else begin this family talk. She'd have plenty to say in her turn.

Ace scratched the side of his head. What was he thinking? There was a little grey in the tidy cut. Would he dye it, she wondered, or go for the distinguished elder look? She coloured her own, just a little, but knew it wouldn't be long before the full works were routine. Well, she had a 17 year old daughter, who was sitting quietly, waiting for the grand inquisitor. Sally was as tall as Ace, slim and lithe. She could be quite beautiful, she could be exceedingly ugly. Sally's make up had been washed off, in tears and soapy water. She had obviously decided that contrition should be plain faced.

'I've the builder coming in...' Ace glanced at his Omega watch, 'thirty two minutes, so let's get going.'

Nadine almost said something about treating the family like a business meeting, but refrained. It was too early for sarcasm.

'You have been expelled from St Anne's, a week ago,' he said to his daughter, 'A full week ago, which you held back from us. I assume that was from a sense of shame.' Ace paused, staring hard at Sally who was looking at her knees. 'Shame at the money I have wasted preparing you for your place in the world. Shame at the horror of this letter.' He shook it and took a breath.

Yes, Nadine noted, he was used to running meetings. Someone should be taking minutes.

'I've read the letter several times. They don't want a drug dealer in the school. That's clear enough. You are a disgrace. But as for your crime, there are no details. For obvious reasons. The school's reputation. It's why they haven't called the police. So you are fortunate. Tell me what you've been doing. No evasions please.'

Sally sniffed, eyes down, she spoke very quietly. 'Mo supplied me. I sold it at school. Only weed, nothing else. For about a month. I didn't make much. I was selling cheap. It wasn't about making money.'

'What was it about?' said Ace.

'I'd been bunking off, the last three months, just going in two or three days a week. They wrote letters home about my absence; I tore them up.'

Ace sighed heavily and shook his head.

'I am so sorry, Dad,' she went on. 'It's like I was taken over by a demon.'

'I don't believe in demonic possession,' he said. 'That is your granny's trope.' He stabbed a finger directly at his daughter's face. 'Whatever you did, you are responsible for. You alone. I will not have you blaming others.'

'I'm not blaming anyone,' she said. 'I knew dealing was wrong. It was so stupid...' She closed her eyes. 'I enjoyed being the bad girl, the one all the girls were talking about. It bigged me up. I could make them wait on me, pick and choose.' She stopped, looked at her mother, not daring to look at her father. 'It was stupid, it was juvenile. I was bound to get caught.'

'That's what I can't understand,' said Ace. 'You are selling weed to schoolgirls. They get stoned. It must be obvious to anyone. They are giggly and stupid. How can someone not notice?'

Sally didn't answer, which Nadine assumed was an acknowledgement of the fact.

'I am stopping your allowance,' said her father. 'You are confined to the house until further notice. I am going to have to tell your grandmother.'

'Please don't, Dad.'

'She must be told,' he said. 'You will be here in the house and not allowed out. Your mother and your grandmother will make sure. I shall confiscate your phone and your laptop. I am not having you communicating with your nefarious associates.'

Sally looked up, appalled.

'What am I going to do?'

'You can read, you can study, you can help your mother in that garden across the road.'

'You can paint and draw,' said Nadine. 'You can play your guitar.'

'So I'm in prison,' said Sally resentfully.

'House arrest,' said Ace. 'Some might say you should be in prison. Be that as it may, you are grounded. Now let's get to the other business...'

On with the agenda, added Nadine silently.

'You are pregnant,' he went on. 'My daughter. Expelled and pregnant. How you have let me down, Sally.'

'I'm sorry, Dad.'

'A little late for apologies. How long? Who?'

'Three months,' said Nadine.

Ace put up a hand to halt his wife. 'Let her tell me please. I want the truth.'

'Three months,' agreed Sally. 'Kingsley is the father.'

'Kingsley who?'

'Kingsley Dayville. Honest. That's a name, I can't forget. I met him at the Shindig.'

'Shindig?' Ace screwed his nose in puzzlement. 'What sort of place is that?'

'That's what Mo and the others called it. The Shindig. These guys all get together in the afternoons, big house, long room, in Plaistow; they play music, smoke weed...'

'And that's where you met this Kingsley Dayville fellow?'

'I was stoned. Strong stuff...' she half smiled then quelled it. 'And well, you know.'

'And what did Mo do about it?'

'He let me do what I wanted.'

'Let me get this straight,' said Ace. 'You should have been at school, but you were bunking off half the time, presumably coming home when expected. And spending your time at the Shindig. Where you smoked dope, and where Dayville took your virginity...'

Nadine rolled her eyes at the quaintness. He was no longer a choir boy. Even he knew, you only lose your virginity once.

Sally nodded. Quaint or not, father and mother had a picture of the Shindig and its goings on. Some variation but a large measure of agreement.

Ace rose from the armchair. 'I want Mo out of the house. All his stuff, I want thrown on the drive. I shall lock the door of his room. Tomorrow, I'll get the builder to change the front door locks. I never want to see that Judas again. Persona non grata. Scum, filth.' He turned to Nadine. 'You have always been his defender.'

She shrugged. 'I was wrong. What else can I say? I knew Mo was a layabout, smoked dope, but I didn't know that he was taking Sally to his dope parties. Let's agree on something. He is scum, filth. Kick him out. I agree one hundred per cent.'

Ace was striding about the room, in old testament prophet mode. He had been betrayed, his hopes for his daughter shattered. But he didn't quite know it all. Sally's dad had to be told.

'We went to BPAS today,' said Nadine.

'And what's that in English?'

'British Pregnancy Advisory Service. Where Sally talked to a counsellor.'

'All this is very speedy. You find out she's pregnant and rush her off to a counsellor. Without thinking to inform me. What did he say, this counsellor?'

'A she. Sally has decided to have an abortion.'

'Did I hear you correctly, Nadine? You have fixed up an abortion.' He was standing over his daughter on the sofa, who was backing off as far as she could. 'And her father, the man who has been paying for her education, giving her an allowance, buying her clothes, is not even to be consulted.'

Nadine knew he would behave this way. It was why she'd taken control.

'She has an appointment for the operation next week,' said Nadine.

'I cannot believe this.' Ace was shaking his hands in disbelief as he strode about the room. 'While I am at work, oblivious, utterly in the dark, her mother conspires with the witches.'

'It was her own decision,' said Nadine. 'Not mine.'

'Rubbish!' He rounded on Sally and clasped both her cheeks between his large hands. 'Do you want an abortion, girl? Tell me.'

'I don't know,' she said feebly.

'You don't know, and yet, with your mother's connivance, one has been arranged.' He let go of Sally and turned to Nadine. 'This is railroading of the worst sort.'

'You are bullying her, Ace. Leave her alone. She's a schoolgirl. Well, she should be. But she has a right to her opinion. It's her body, not yours.'

'Do you want an abortion, Sally?' said her father.

'I don't know,' she said barely audibly, eyes closed.

'Then we shall cancel the appointment.'

'You can't,' exclaimed Nadine. 'It's her decision.'

'The operation shall be cancelled. Do you agree with me, Sally?'

He waited, standing over her, demanding. Nadine knew her daughter couldn't take his force.

'Yes,' came a diminutive voice. 'I agree.'

As expected. What could Nadine do or say in this hurricane? Perhaps take her off secretly... Don't fight him.

'We'll cancel it first thing tomorrow,' said Ace.

There was a ring of the doorbell.

'Ah, the builder, I am sure. Well, we have finished here. And on time. I am fully in the picture and we know what we are doing. Come on, Sally, let's go upstairs so your mother can't cast another spell on you.'

Chapter 16

Jack had come with Mia. It was still warm out, and he was wearing a faded, much worn t-shirt with his jeans. He didn't expect it to be a long session with Ace. Mia could have a chat with the daughter while he did the business. What was the girl's name? He couldn't recall. Last time he'd seen her, she'd been weeping with her mother in the community garden. What had that been about?

Mia hadn't objected to coming, being curious about the girl, only a couple of years older, who went to a posh school. Was she really clever, with all that expensive education, or just posh?

The door was opened by Ace, his daughter a little way down the hallway.

'Hello, Jack. Do come in.'

'I've brought my daughter,' he said. 'I hope you don't mind.'

'Fine, fine.' He turned to Sally. 'I'm sure you can entertain Jack's daughter. Take her up to your room. And mind what I've said. I don't want you talking to your mother. Do you understand me?'

'Yes, Dad.' She turned to Mia. 'Come on, we'll go to my room.'

Mia followed Sally up the stairs. Jack went with Ace along the hallway and into the kitchen, curious about the order given to Sally not to talk to her mother. Strange request. Never? Just tonight? A power battle, with the kid in the middle. Well, hardly kid, young lady almost.

Ace halted by the area of the island, delineated on the floorboards with masking tape. It was crossed by five parallel lines of tape, each representing a joist beneath the boards.

'So what is the problem, Jack?'

'The two ends of the island are not resting on joists.' Jack pointed to one end. 'Here. See?' He walked along the length of the putative island. 'And here.'

'Why is that a problem?'

'The weight of the island,' said Jack. 'Bricks are heavy. Unsupported, the floorboards could collapse under the weight.'

Ace examined the contour of the island, scratching his head as he shuffled from one end to the other.

'How likely is that?' he said.

Jack shrugged. 'I don't know. There's the risk. But if we moved the island. To there.' He indicated where. 'Then this end is resting on a joist. And, if we make the island eight inches shorter, then that end would be on one too.' He took a couple of steps to the other end.

'Enough,' said Ace, shaking his head. 'I don't want it moved.'

'Alright. Same place, then we make both ends longer.'

'I am satisfied with the length. You are a builder, Jack. Not an engineer. I don't believe there's much likelihood of a collapse.'

'Maybe not immediately, but perhaps in three or four years...'

'I won't be here in three or four years. Enough. Go away and get a college degree.'

Jack stiffened, wanting to argue, but the man with the money was calling the shots. As always.

'Get on with it,' went on Ace. 'Make the island. Exactly as laid out in the plan. And no more shilly shallying. You have lost more than half a day. I am annoyed by all this questioning.'

'I had to ask,' said Jack, flattened by power.

'And the reply is carry on. Look here, Jack, I am paying you by the day, and all I have got so far is lines of masking tape on the floor.'

'I thought there was a risk,' said Jack.

'I had already considered it. And decided it was most unlikely. I insist you get on with the work first thing tomorrow. Lay them damn bricks, and no more time wasting. And what's more... I will be deducting half a day's money. You'll get one hundred and fifty tomorrow.'

'This should have been sorted out over the phone,' said Jack, trying to keep his temper. 'But you told me to stop work and come back at 9.30.'

'Do you want this job or not?'

One of those moments. A direct challenge. He'd like nothing more than to walk away. But he had no other work and too many debts.

'I'll get moving tomorrow,' he said.

'Good. And if you do a long day, I'll pay you in full. Is that fair?'

'Yes, Mr Baldwin.' What else could he say? That he felt screwed?

'And now, I want to know about my wife. Let's go outside. Just in case there are eavesdroppers.'

Jack followed Ace through the garden door onto the patio, thinking about the next day's labour. There was no way he could make the work up tomorrow as he had Mia to look after, so working late wasn't on the cards. But this wasn't the time or place to tell Ace. He wanted to go right now, he'd been belittled enough. Just get away from the man. But there was the spying aspect of the job, for which his payment had been bumped up. What on earth was he going to say?

They sat at the ironwork table. Ace had closed the kitchen door, so as not to be overheard. The sun was setting, and the horizon was aglow, the clouds fringed with yellow and flaming red.

Ace had his back to the sun, his face in deep shadow, barely visible.

'Have you anything to report about my wife's activities?'

'I have,' said Jack, his mind whirring with possibilities. What, what, what?

'So let me hear.'

'I'll tell you exactly what,' said Jack tentatively, 'if I get full payment for tomorrow. And in advance.'

It was one hell of a try on. He might just get sacked on the spot. Not that he knew what he was going to tell the irate husband. That he was considering an affair with Nadine? No, sir.

'Tell me now,' said Ace impatiently. 'I'll judge whether it's worth the money.'

'It is worth the money,' said Jack. 'Most definitely. But payment first. Then I'll tell you.'

'You're broke,' said Ace irately. 'You're in debt up to your ears. You have no other work.'

'And I have valuable information.'

He'd gone too far to back out. The worst that could happen is that he'd be fired. And money or not, he might just go for it. At least, he could pursue an affair with Nadine without betraying his employer, who would have sacked him if he found out. And deserve it too. That was if Jack had an affair with Nadine. It might just be a flirtation in her eyes.

'Suppose your information isn't worth the money,' said Ace, 'and I've paid you for junk?'

'Then make a deduction, the day after tomorrow.'

'I could,' said Ace thoughtfully. 'You're right. Astute. I like that. That's why I employed you. But enough, enough.' He rose. 'Stay there. It had better be good, what you have to say. Your job's on the line.'

Ace left him and went into the kitchen.

Jack was half amused by the situation. Too broke to be fully amused. He might be out of a job in the next few minutes. He'd done next to no work today, but whose fault was that? Ace could have said 'carry on' over the phone. But the busy man can't do anything so simple.

Enough. Forget the gripes about the job. The man has to have some scandalous info on Nadine.

What a day! He'd lumbered Nadine with a thousand pound fine. That might kill his chances with her anyway. Though need he tell her? Concentrate, one problem at a time. He was so easily distracted. What on earth was he going to say to Ace? It was hard work being a spy. Payment by results. He had to come up with something.

The sun had set. It was darker, but not fully dark. In that twilight with the sun gone down, but close enough to the horizon for light to spill over. Not really telescope time. These summer nights barely got fully dark. Once the sun has set, it was contemplating rising. The bane of astronomers.

Ace returned. He slapped a bundle of cash on the table. 'There's three hundred, you crook. What's she up to?'

Jack flicked through the notes, but wasn't counting it; he needed the time. He pocketed the money. He was as nervous as if he'd been asked to give a speech to a hall of five hundred. He kept his hands below the table, so Ace wouldn't see them shaking. He pressed them to his knees.

'She's having an affair,' he said.

'I thought so.' Ace rubbed his hand. 'Tell me about him.'

'It's a woman.'

Ace sucked in his breath. 'That surprises me. It shouldn't. But it does. Well, well. That explains a lot.'

'A white woman.'

'A white woman even?' He paused and eyed Jack. 'How do you know?'

'I went downstairs to get the keys for the side garden door. And I heard them at it.'

'Really going at it?'

'Hammer and tongs. Heavy breathing, cries. I left them to it and went outside. In the drive, I piled bricks in the wheelbarrow until the woman came out. She came up the basement steps.'

'She would. Not wanting to be seen by anyone in the house.'

'She ignored me totally when I said good morning. I watched her, but she didn't turn back to look at me. She walked down the side road by the community garden. I went to my van, pretended to be getting some tools out, so I could keep a watch. She went in the side gate of the garden. She had a key.'

Ace let out a breath as if he'd been holding it.

'One of the garden group,' he exclaimed. 'I should have suspected it. This woman... Tell me, what did she look like?'

'Short, blonde, mid to late 30s I'd say.'

'I know the one. Oh yes, I know the one. Talks a lot. Laughs all the time. They come over here for meetings sometimes. Hippy lot. Sleep around like alley cats.'

They didn't speak for a minute. Jack had told his tale and both were considering its implications. Jack the lies, and Ace the who and how of the alley cat.

'Excuse me asking,' said Jack. Ace was a silhouette in the growing gloom, darkening trees and houses behind him. 'You're divorcing. Why does it matter what your wife is doing?'

Ace stiffened. 'She remains my wife, Jack. Forever my wife. Always. It's difficult to explain to a non believer. I am assuming you are not religious. Fewer and fewer people are these days. We were married in church. Marriage vows should be honoured. You marry once in the eyes of God. You stay married.'

'Are you a Catholic?'

He nodded. 'You marry once. You stay married. Till the end of time.'

Chapter 17

Mia was sitting on the bed looking about the room, Sally on a chair. There were posters on the wall, mostly black pop singers, but one of a woman footballer. Megan Rapinoe, the US team captain.

'She's great,' said Mia. 'Talks back. She won't be put down.'

'Scores goals. Won't have racism. Or sexism. She's a player.'

'Nice room,' said Mia. 'Got your own TV and sound system. Do you play that guitar?'

'Not a lot, but I guess I will be.' She shrugged. 'I've been grounded. Big Daddy has spoken.' She smiled brightly. 'They think they know so much. But they messed up the world for us. Climate change, pollution, and think they can still order us around like chess pieces.'

Mia was a little surprised by the tirade. It wasn't as if the black girl in front of her had her own money. All the stuff in this room was paid for, plus her posh school, by 'Big Daddy'. She wasn't quite the victim she was claiming. Though, she'd evidently been up to something.

'Why have you been grounded?' she said.

Sally bit her finger, considering.

'Everyone is going to know soon enough,' she said with a long sigh. 'Including Granny. And won't she go on and on.' She imitated a Jamaican accent. 'Come with me to church, child. Read your bible every day. From Genesis to Revelations, my girl. Read and learn, save your soul.'

'You have some sins to confess?' Mia eyed her with a half smile.

'In thought, word and deed, baby. Oh yes, I have sinned. Where shall I begin?' She paused for effect. 'I've been expelled from school. St Anne's. Out in Essex. Stuffy place. All rules. The only thing I liked there was music and football. I was dealing weed. They think,' she pointed through the floorboards, 'I was just doing it for a month. More like three months.'

'Wow,' exclaimed Mia. 'You were bound to get caught.'

'I knew it. But I liked the excitement. Being at the centre of things. The girls kept asking me for a deal. I loved fooling all those bossy teachers. They treat you like kids. It's a prison. You're held in this regime. Go here, do this, do that. Line up, no talking, phones away. Go to assembly, write, read, sing. And here I was breaking all the rules.'

'But you got caught. And they've expelled you.'

'Good riddance to St Anne's. I'll be the story there for a century.'

Mia wondered whether she would. Other girls would be expelled. And dealing was only dealing. Still, Mia was in Sally's space and not about to argue with her. She could sympathise with the 'school as prison' metaphor.

What you have to put up with to get an education.

'And I'm pregnant.'

That was more of a shocker. Posh girl in the pudding club.

'Are you really?'

'Three months.'

She certainly had a need to impress, thought Mia. She had known her less than quarter of an hour, and knew she was expelled from school for dealing and pregnant. But Sally hadn't asked a thing about her.

'How did that happen?'

'Usual way.' She laughed. 'Haven't they shown you the movies yet?'

'Seen a couple. I know what goes where. They do say use a condom. But not at St Anne's, I would think, being a Catholic school.'

'Condoms are a sin. And I am a sinner. I've been expelled from Eden.'

'Are you going to have the baby?'

'There's a good question for a summer evening.' She smirked. 'Mummy says have an abortion, Daddy says that's wickedness.'

'What do you say?'

'Do I really want a screaming brat? Be someone's mummy, wiping its bum, changing its nappies.' She blew a raspberry, reflecting on the opposing scenarios. 'Me and Mum fixed up an appointment at an abortion clinic for next week. Dad says it's got to be cancelled.'

'What do you say?'

'I say Daddy has the money round here. Mummy makes next to nothing with her painting and the community garden pittance. They're divorcing, but she's still living in his house. He's worth a lot, gonna be even richer the hours he works. And I am his only child. Do I want to toe the line and have his grandchild? What would you do?'

'Not get pregnant.'

'Smart kid.' She nodded. 'But the limits of a Catholic education leave you a little unprepared...'

'Not all Catholic girls get pregnant. I am sure quite a few know what a condom is. Or the morning after pill.'

'And I do too. But I got awfully stoned, and I didn't care. You see? There's a theme in my life. Up to now anyway. Not caring. It got me expelled, it got me pregnant. If I have an abortion Daddy and Granny will have a go at me for the rest of my life. If I don't I've got a brat on my hands. See my problem?'

'Yep. Sure do.' She wondered what Jack and Alison would do in that situation. 'It's not a free choice, is it?'

'Not unless I want to run away to sea.' She paused. 'Let's push that into a corner and talk about how you can help me.'

'How I can help?' said Mia cautiously, wondering what devious activity Sally had in mind for her. She wasn't going to be dealing dope. No way.

'Well, I told you I've been grounded,' said Sally. 'The muggles have taken away my phone and laptop, just to make sure I am thoroughly miserable.'

'To stop you getting corrupted further.'

'Too late for that. Hang about.'

She rose, picked up a pair of scissors from her dresser and went to a corner of the room. Sally got down on her knees, and with a point of the scissors, she eased up a short floor board. Taking it out, she put her arm into the space, and with some effort pulled out a bulging cloth bag.

'My ill gotten gains,' said Sally.

She took the bag to the bed and emptied it out. There were bundles of banknotes tied up with elastic bands.

'This your drugs money?' said Mia, appalled and impressed.

'Yes. There's £900 odd here.' She picked up some bundles and packed them together. 'This is 500 quid. Take it. There's two hundred for your trouble.'

Mia backed off.

'I'm not dealing drugs. No way.'

'No, no, nothing illegal. I've done that already. I want you to buy me a phone and a tablet. Say a hundred for the phone, say two hundred for the tablet. And the rest is for you.'

Mia was sucking her lip. No lawbreaking. Easy money. Just some shopping, and parents to fool. For two hundred quid.

'How do I get the money out of here? I haven't got a bag with me.'

'And I can't lend you one. I'm in disgrace. They'll suspect something. It'll have to be pockets, socks, knickers, bra. I'm sure we can stuff it in. I want you to buy the gear tomorrow. Can you? And no rubbish.'

Mia shrugged. 'I know what's what. I can take the day off. We're not doing anything at school. End of term stuff.'

'The community garden is open tomorrow,' said Sally. 'My mum goes in to organise things. I shall ask if I can help her. I'm sure she'll agree. I can say I want to do some sketching. She likes me doing that. And that's how you'll get the tablet and phone to me. I'll try to be there at one o'clock. So you be there then. If for any reason, I'm not, then I want you to put them in a plastic bag. And put it under the shipping container, near its doors. Got that?'

'That's easy enough.'

'OK. Remember, no rubbish. Let's get this money on you, before you have to go.

Chapter 18

'Good to hear you've got troubles too, bro,' said Nick. 'That almost cheers me up.'

He, Ace and their mother were in the sitting room. The TV was off. Nick had not left his armchair. Marta and Ace were on the long sofa.

'I cannot believe it of the girl,' said Marta. She had put down her knitting, unable to concentrate. 'Such a disgrace to bring on the family. Expelled for dealing drugs. And, as if that is not enough, pregnant too. She will come to church with me on Sunday and make her confession.'

'Too late for that,' said Nick with a smirk.

'Never too late,' said Marta. 'But tell me again. What's all this about an abortion? Nadine rushing the girl to one of those places. She would of course. That's her way.'

'I'll cancel it tomorrow,' said Ace. 'Sally will have the baby. We can get an au pair or a nanny when it's born.'

'We don't need them,' protested Marta. 'It's only a baby. What's the girl going to be doing?'

'Getting on with her education. I still want her going to university. For the time being, she's grounded. No phone, no laptop. Nadine accepts the need for punishment. One of the few things we agree on. Please make sure Sally doesn't go out.'

'Here we go,' exclaimed Nick. 'Ace the arranger. What he wants, how he sets it all up. Except Sally didn't play his game. Good for her!'

'I'm sure you'd love your Liz to be expelled and pregnant.'

Nick leaped from his chair. 'You leave my family out of this, you dog turd. You've done them enough damage already.'

'With you totally innocent in the matter, of course.'

'I am going to kill you, Ace. You know that, I am going to squeeze the fat life out of your smug face.'

He was standing over his brother, clenching his fists. Ace's hands were ready if he made a move.

Marta rose and stood between them.

'Stop it. How is this any help?' she declared, pushing Nick away. 'You wind him up too easily, Ace. And you react as if you are a clockwork toy, Nick. You are family, both of you. Enough of this fighting.'

Nick backed further away, going to the front window, the curtains still open in the twilight.

'Mo is the villain now,' he said with a chuckle. 'Or the hero, depending on your point of view.'

'That dealer is out the house,' exclaimed Ace. 'I want no one to let him in. You hear!'

'Suppose I do,' said Nick teasingly. 'What then?'

'He won't dare come back here. And you, you've got your own place. Why are you here to taunt me?'

Nick turned from the window.

'You can throw me out too, big brother. Show everyone what a great bouncer you are.'

'Then Mo can live with you,' said Ace. 'Run his drug dealing from your house. Make you some money, smart guy. I hear you're in need of that.'

Nick ran in, fists up. Marta stopped him, arms wide.

'Please cease this,' exclaimed Marta. 'You can't be in the same room together. Always fighting, from when you were kids.'

All three were standing, she was between her sons like a fence. They like stags, displaying. With too much history for either to back down.

'I'm putting all Mo's stuff out on the drive,' said Ace. 'Anyone going to help?'

'I'll help,' said Marta. 'That boy is beyond the pale.'

'Not me,' said Nick. 'I'm cheering on the prodigal son.'

Ace bit his lip but said nothing. He left the room, followed by Marta.

Chapter 19

In the morning, it was pouring with rain, while Jack and Mia were having breakfast. Through the kitchen window, he watched the puddles filling. The water barrels in the community garden would have been filling too, that is if they hadn't been filled already, at an unholy cost. He'd been caught, gave a fake name, but someone would have to pay. Surely not him? He was just helping out.

Accessory. Wasn't that the word?

Not the word. He didn't have to connect the water. Nadine couldn't, and so she asked him to and he agreed. The desire to impress. To save the garden. Superman! Except that wasn't the word, as he'd collapsed. If he hadn't, there was a good chance the barrels would have been filled and the hose disconnected before the man came. If he'd just eaten the way he had been told to.

Not accessory. Guilty, your honour. I did it with my wrench and jubilee clips. And lousy diet.

The sky was deep grey; there was more rain up there yet. He concentrated on a puddle on the back garden path, rain drops pinging its surface, splattering upwards for an instant, and then engulfed by the mass. What made a cloud drop its load? Why here, when it has travelled so far from the sea?

Any thought but the thought that the community garden would have to pay the £1000 fine due. He should've looked at the weather forecast before connecting the hose yesterday. But done. Too late for ifs and ands. He should tell Nadine.

But would he?

Jack turned away from the window, and offered to drive Mia to school, but she said she'd take an umbrella and get the bus. That was fine by Jack as his van was up the road anyway. She wouldn't get that wet. It was summer rain, warm, not the chilling wetness of a winter's day. And lots of buses this time of the morning.

Mia had made him a grapefruit and muesli with banana. He said 'very nice, very colourful' when he saw it on the kitchen table. There wasn't any bacon anyway for his preferred breakfast: cholesterol on toast, sunny side up. Mia quickly ate and left. A music rehearsal, she said. It was only when she was out of the house that he remembered he hadn't given her lunch money.

He phoned.

'Come back,' he said. 'I haven't given you any money for your lunch.'

'I'm at the bus stop. There's a bus coming right now. I've got money anyway. Don't worry.'

Mia hung up. He'd pay her back tonight.

Jack made himself a cheese sandwich for lunch, put a lettuce leaf between the slices to make it healthy looking, though he knew it didn't work that way. But a bit of green was better than no green. Slightly less chance of getting scurvy, though how much vitamin C was in a lettuce? He needed something for mid morning. He took a couple of bananas and an apple. This was dreadful. Rabbit food. A red blooded builder can't live on this.

He had money and so could go out for lunch. No, he mustn't. He'd only get junk. He left the money he'd finagled out of Ace in a drawer, though he needed to bank it. Tomorrow. Tonight, he'd make a list of his debts and sort out who to pay first.

Jack was ready to leave, lunch in his backpack, when he saw two twenty pound notes on the carpet. That was careless of him; comes of being paid in cash. Should he put that in the drawer too?

He pocketed the notes and left the flat.

The rain had eased up. It was a soft drizzle, though he put his hood up and walked rapidly to work. Only just down the road. Must get the bricklaying on the move this morning. And develop the tale for Ace: Nadine and her blond lover from the community garden. Keep it believable, not too fantastic. Should he tell her? And add the slight detail of the fine from the water board. Secrets already, and he'd only known her a day. She'd have some too. They'd hardly had time to come clean.

Though who tells the whole truth? Ever. As soon as you learn to talk, you learn to lie. Teddy ate the biscuit.

Teddy connected the hose.

She was divorcing, so an affair would be OK. Sort of. Just a string of lies for his employer, which might yet come to haunt him. Ace was a difficult man, once he had made his mind up. The daughter had some troubles. He wondered what. Nadine had been consoling her in the community garden. She was the co-ordinator or something. It was her, Eve in the garden, who'd got him to connect the hose.

Not Teddy.

He could've said no. But they'd shared a moment, an hour earlier. A one off, or more to come? He didn't know, but certainly wanted to.

Jack arrived at his van, outside the house. He opened up and left his backpack on the seat. The rain was so slight, he decided to leave his jacket there too. He considered getting a wheelbarrow out and his bricklaying tools, but decided he wanted a last look at the island. Besides, he needed the side door to be open to bring the gear through to the patio.

Jack was climbing the house steps as Ace was coming through the front door. He was smart and sombre in a long grey coat, holding a black umbrella up. About to close the front door, he left it open for Jack.

'Must rush,' he said, coming down the stairs. 'Train to catch. Sally will be around today. Don't let her bother you. And don't lend her your phone.'

'OK,' he said, puzzled.

'One more thing, I've thrown Mo out. Never mind why. Don't let him back in. Not for anything.' And then Ace was away, calling back, 'And lay them bricks.'

Jack watched him striding down the road in his polished black leather shoes. As if off to a funeral, but no: a train to catch, money to be made. Sally must have had her phone confiscated. Some bad behaviour. Was Mo connected? The girl had been weeping yesterday with Nadine. What did teenage girls get up to? He should know, being the father of one. Shoplifting? Not likely. Ace would give her plenty of spending money. Cheating at exams or bullying. Drugs? Getting pregnant? Well, Nadine had rushed her off. And there were some associates who mustn't be contacted by phone.

That was it, he reckoned. He'd bet on it. She was up the duff. Jack could make light of it as it wasn't Mia, and he was still smarting from the telling off by Ace yesterday.

In the hallway, coats on the hooks, but no bike today. Someone loaned it to someone, stolen or what? More room if he had to bring anything in this way. Though the garden door would be a lot easier and less mess.

Jack went into the kitchen. Sally was making toast, wearing a t-shirt and jeans torn at the knee. She was bare footed, her toenails painted deep red.

Jack saw at once his masking tape was scuffed, some coming off the floor. The kitchen had a lot of traffic, no point getting irked. Easily fixed.

'Hello, Jack,' said Sally chirpily, leaving off buttering. 'Can I borrow your phone?'

Good job he'd been warned.

'Your dad says no. I mustn't part with it.' He paused and added. 'Part of your punishment.'

'He told you about it, did he?'

'He did.' Not that he had, but Jack hoped to learn more, being a curious soul.

'He's telling everyone,' she went on. 'Granny's already had a go at me. Wants to drag me off to confession.'

'Will you go?'

'Not if I can help it.'

He wondered why she wasn't at school. If she was pregnant, she wasn't showing, and so could go in. There was more to this.

'And trouble at school too,' he said.

'I'm glad that's done with,' she said. 'Finito. The end. Like a jail house, that place. Never ending homework. All the assemblies. Dress codes.' She laughed. 'Being expelled is not a punishment. It's early release.'

He couldn't help a smile, remembering his own feelings. That last year at school, he'd been more out then in. But he wasn't expelled. Close, but he had been saved that indignity.

Jack got down on his knees and went round pressing down the masking tape. Some of it would have to be renewed. There aren't many things you get expelled for, he reflected. Stealing? Not likely. Vandalism? Possible. Drugs? Had to be.

'Was Mo supplying you?' he said, concentrating on the errant tape.

'Good old Uncle Mo,' she said. 'Dad's kicked him out. My dealer and my pimp. You shocked?'

'Yes. I am.'

'Not actually my pimp. I wasn't selling myself, just having a good time.'

'When's the baby due?'

A guess on the fly. He could always pretend it was a joke.

She shrugged. 'Ages and ages.' She was buttering the toast.

He'd reckoned right. A lot to take in. Girl at posh school, selling drugs and pregnant. Expelled and grounded. He noted there was no talk of the police. Posh schools don't like that. Lucky for her.

'I liked your daughter, Mia,' she said. 'She's smart. Smarter than me.'

I should hope so, thought Jack.

'I'd better bring in some bricks,' he said, looking again at the tape. He'd better get a roll from the van and fix those bits that weren't staying down.

'Got any advice for me?' said Sally. She took a bite of toast. 'Everyone else has.'

'Not my place,' he said. 'You're not my daughter.' Though he could have said, get some contraception and better friends.

Instead, he said, 'Where's your bike?'

'In the hall.'

'No, it isn't.'

She ran out into the hall, and yelled to the house, 'Who's got my bike?'

That would waken the dead. Not his problem though. So, tape and bring bricks and mortar in, spirit level, trowel, bucket and line. Bound to forget something. That was always the way.

Nadine came in with Sally. Her presence electrified him. Her figure, her face, her being. The smile she gave him, so welcoming, it hollowed his legs.

'No, I don't know anything about your bike, Sally. I haven't ridden it in weeks.'

'Then where is it? Someone must know.'

'Why me?'

'My bike's missing and you just don't care. Typical!'

She went running out, presumably to blame someone else, thought Jack.

'Good morning, Jack,' she said. 'Sorry about my daughter, but I have had more than enough of her. I have no idea where her bike is. And I really don't care. Families!' She beamed at him, a shared happiness. 'I'm in the community garden today. It's open to the public. All that carry-on with the water yesterday. Quite ironic, with the rain we've had. But how was I to know?' She shrugged. 'Doesn't matter.'

Oh yes it does, he thought.

'I need the keys to the side door to bring the bricks to the patio,' he said.

She took a bunch of keys from the pocket of her jeans and threw them over. Same keys he'd had yesterday, for the community garden as well as the back door here. Last night, he'd pushed them through her letter box when leaving with Mia.

'Give 'em back soon as you've finished.' From across the room, she was gazing out of the window, the drips running down the glass. 'I want it to rain, then I want it to stop. See? Never satisfied. You must come over to the garden later. Maybe have your lunch there. If it's raining, there's shelter, but it looks like it's stopping. So come.'

'Why not,' he said and headed for the back garden door.

'I'll make you a coffee.'

'Great.' He was going to say two sugars, but stopped himself. All these waymarkers in a day. No sugar was one of them.

Lunch with Nadine in the garden. A more positive waymarker. He looked forward to it.

Jack stepped outside. It was raining slightly, not enough to bother him. There was a patch of blue in the sky. Likely it would be clearing. Hopefully, all gone by his lunchtime tryst. But for the time being, he would hardly get wet, working mostly inside. All he had to do was pick up the bricks and mortar, and a few tools, then it'd be inside work.

He almost tripped over Mo.

He was lying on the ground, half curled up on his side, in a pool of blood. Jack bent down and touched his forehead. It was cold and pale. His eyes were wide open, glazed. Flies had settled on a large red patch on his back, soaking through his jacket.

Jack shivered, breath coming quickly. Mo was clearly dead. Jack supported himself on the garden table. The drained face, the lips barely pink, almost asleep, if he wasn't so pale... A man he'd first met out here yesterday morning. Dead. The one who'd been kicked out for supplying Sally.

What had he said, some old fashioned expression? Sitting on that seat eating toast, laughing. Dance for the organ grinder. That was it.

Poor guy.

Jack would not be dancing for any grinder today. Work was done for. Once the word was out to the world. Mo is dead. Get a grip. He must move. The man is dead. Must share.

What a world! Full of surprises.

Jack poked his head in the kitchen. Nadine was putting coffee in the cafetière.

'Mo's out here. On the patio,' he said. 'Dead. We've got to call the police.'

Chapter 20

They were in the sitting room, waiting to be called, like errant students outside the principal's office. A uniformed policewoman was with them, seated on a wooden chair, giving her charges the softer seats. The house had been taken over. Through the window, they could see asexual figures coming and going to their vehicles, clothed in white plastic from head to foot, with masks over their faces.

Nick had commandeered his armchair. Marta had the other, her face red with weeping. Jack, Nadine and Sally sat on the long sofa. All focused on the TV, which was off. This was no time for quizzes and soaps.

'I cannot believe this,' said Marta wiping her eyes. 'I simply cannot believe what is going on in the world.'

'Just look out the window,' said Nick, drumming his fingers on the seat arm. 'All those cops. Busy, busy, busy. Our taxes. Do they need so many?'

Nadine looked at her watch and sighed. She said to the policewoman, 'I have to be in the community garden in an hour.'

'I'll see what I can do,' she said.

'Thank you,' said Nadine. 'I appreciate it.' She turned to Jack and said in a low voice, 'I wonder if you could come over the garden with me. There's a job there, as you can't do anything here.' She stopped. 'You must think me callous, but Mo is Mo. And well...' She hesitated. 'I'll tell you about it later.'

He knew more than she realised. 'I'll come,' he said. He owed her that, and more, thinking of the fine he'd hit the garden with.

'The world must go on,' said Nick. 'Flowers gotta grow, frogs gotta croak.'

'He was stabbed,' said Sally sullenly. 'All that blood. A kitchen knife, I bet you anything.'

Nadine and Sally had come out onto the garden when Jack told them of Mo's death. He'd tried to hold them back, but they'd pushed past him to see for themselves. Though he had managed to get them back into the kitchen, once they'd seen the worst, to drink coffee, consider their own mortality and wait for the law.

'Who killed cock robin? The one who hated him the most,' said Nick. 'Obvious. So, take your pick. Just one missing though, to complete the set. The main man.'

'I've called Ace,' said Marta. 'He must be here. They'll want to talk to him. He is catching the train back.'

'Such a shock,' said Nadine, her hands to her cheeks. 'And here's me thinking of going to the community garden, when out there on the patio... I couldn't believe it. Mo was always larger than life.'

'The youngest of me boys going first.' Marta sniffed and dabbed her eyes. 'This should not have happened.'

'Lots of things shouldn't have happened,' said Nick, throwing up his arms. 'I shouldn't be in this house, Sally shouldn't be pregnant...'

'Shut up,' snapped Nadine.

'It's only the truth,' he said. 'Has to be faced.'

'Says a man who looked truth in the eye,' said Nadine.

Nick threw his head back and chuckled mirthlessly. 'Well you may lecture me, sister-in-law. You certainly have in the past. All your environmental flimflam. But let it be said, if you and Ace hadn't been so busy arguing you might have noticed your daughter was going astray.'

100

'Good advice from a bankrupt shopkeeper,' said Nadine.

'What do you think of my family?' said Sally mock brightly, to Jack.

'It's not my place to make judgements,' he said.

'I bet you are making them, though,' she said.

He was, he couldn't not be. Likely the killer was in this room, or it could be Ace who was on his way. How could he not judge, even though he'd only known them a day or so. Not quite true. He'd known Nick too long. Ace he'd met in the evening on the Flats, less than two days ago. The others yesterday morning. And he hadn't laid a single brick. That's what he was here for. And oh yes, to tell lies about Nadine. Though, he'd had eight hundred pounds in payment, that was a great joke, with not a single, solitary brick laid. He could hardly believe it. If you ripped the masking tape off the floorboards, you wouldn't know he'd been here at all.

Crime Scene investigators were out on the patio and garden being drizzled on. They were in the kitchen, and here and there in the house, all togged up like zombies. A takeover as if they now owned the house. Which in a sense they did. Murder gave them ownership.

When would he be working again?

How practical! His callousness was a match for Nadine's. But Mo was dead; there was no calling him back. Jack barely knew him. He had been alive, he was now a corpse. Almost like a figure on the news, if Jack hadn't had a brief conversation with him. Seen him eating toast and laughing. But that was yesterday, all gone, driven away with the blade of a knife.

A young, uniformed policeman entered.

'Jack Bell?' he said.

'Me,' said Jack.

'They're ready for you now, sir, if you'd like to come with me.'

Jack rose, relieved to be leaving the room. It was like a funeral, without the sandwiches and wine. He was only a builder, here by accident, a little sad. They were family, with real emotions. Or faked.

The police constable led him down the stairs. Jack had been this way yesterday morning with Nadine. Her bedroom and studio doors were closed this morning. He followed the constable along the downstairs hallway to the end door.

'Just go in. They're expecting you.'

Jack entered a small sitting room. Two people were present, both plain clothes officers sitting side by side on a sofa. He knew them both.

'Hello, Jack, Fancy meeting you here.'

This was Fayyad, who Jack knew was a detective sergeant at Forest Gate police station. An old friend from school.

Fayyad held his hand out and Jack shook it.

'We keep bumping into each other,' said Jack.

'Small world, Forest Gate. You know Hayley?'

'Sure,' said Jack. 'Your regular partner.'

She smiled. Hayley was tall and slim, in brown trousers and a green shirt, hair very short. Fayyad was in a blue grey suit. He'd unbuttoned the jacket but that was as far as he'd go now that he was a sergeant.

'How long have you been working here, Jack?'

'Since yesterday morning. I met Ace Baldwin the night before to set up the job. And Nick Baldwin, well, I worked for him for 6 weeks and he went bankrupt on me. He owes me three thousand quid for wages and materials. And I won't get a penny.'

'That's bad luck,' said Fayyad. 'Had you met Mo at all?'

'Once, yesterday morning, for maybe ten minutes. I was on the patio going through the plans. I'm here to build an island in the kitchen. You know, one of those table-cum-workspaces that posh people have.'

'I've got one,' interjected Fayyad. 'I'm not posh.'

'Says you.' They were old pals. Jack could get away with it.

'What did you think of Mo?'

'Happy go lucky, you might say. Lived on his wits. He got up late yesterday morning. I liked him face to face, liked him less the more I heard about him.'

Jack told them what he knew about Mo's dealing and his part in Sally getting expelled and pregnant. Hayley was taking notes.

'Ace kicked him out,' said Jack.

'So what was he doing back again?'

'Well, all I can say is he didn't have a key,' said Jack. 'He told me Ace wouldn't give him one.'

Fayyad looked at Hayley.

'There wasn't one on him,' she said. 'They've only found a phone and a little money on the body. No key.'

'Someone must've let him in,' said Fayyad. 'I wonder who that might have been.'

Chapter 21

After his interview, Jack was free to go. As he was leaving the detectives, he told them that Nadine had to open the community garden soon. Fayyad and Hayley agreed she could be next. Jack went up the stairs with the young duty cop. He waited in the hallway while Nadine was called.

'See you in the garden,' he said to her when she came out.

'I hope I won't be too long,' she said. 'I hate these things.'

There was no possibility of any intimacy with the constable present. Nadine went down the stairs, Jack left by the front door which was open to facilitate the comings and goings of the forensic investigators. There would be time, he told himself. He and she'd be in the garden together. Lots to be said.

A crime scene officer came up the outside stairs as he was going out the front door. He said hello, the zombie mumbled something back. A man or woman? In that shapeless white outfit, totally enclosing the body from head to foot, hood up and masked, any clues of sex were well hidden.

The rain had stopped, the sun out in a cloudy sky. Jack looked at his watch. Not ten yet. It felt such a long morning. Another universe when he'd arrived and talked to Sally. So many people since. Such a shake up.

He looked at the house side door, the one to the garden. The door he was going to open when he'd found Mo. She had the keys again. Back and forth. The garden door was

104

between two houses, the neighbour's back door beside it, separated by a fence. The door was standard height, with a couple of feet of wood above it. The same on the other door. Jack couldn't imagine Mo scaling that. He'd probably have been half stoned anyway. So someone had let him in, either by the front door or by the side door.

Or Nadine's door. He'd forgotten that one. But if he'd have come in through Nadine's he'd would have to come upstairs and go through the kitchen to the patio. And risk being seen. Ace had kicked Mo out, so coming in the garden door would attract the least attention. If he was right, that cut things down somewhat. Who had a key to the side door? He knew Nadine did. Anyone else?

Jack went to his van and sat in the cab ruminating. Ace would have one. It was his house. Maybe Marta. Sally not likely. Could be there was a spare on a hook somewhere. Some people did that in houses he'd worked in, though he hadn't seen one here.

How long would her questioning be? Half an hour perhaps. Difficult to say, depends how thorough they were going to be. All of them would have to go the station for a full interview. These were preliminary.

Jack would go tomorrow. He wasn't important, not a suspect, he could tell by the informality of his interview. More of a chat than pointed questioning. He was just a builder, here for a job.

Taking out the contents of his backpack, Jack contemplated what to eat. Two bananas, an apple and two cheese sandwiches, and a bottle of tap water. He had forty quid in his pocket. He could go over the Forest Cafe and have a proper breakfast.

Jack ate a banana. No, no, not this rabbit food. He was out of the cab and striding up the road. Nothing would halt him. He had decided. A decent breakfast.

At the Forest Cafe, Jack ordered a bacon sandwich and a mug of tea. He ate it there with lashings of mustard on the pink flesh. Feeling better for it. Feeling worse for it. He should have left the forty quid at home. He was too easily tempted.

He walked back. At least he'd eaten, even if he'd sinned. He'd stay upright.

Jack sat in the van. The sun was shining, the clouds white and spaced with lots of blue. That was probably the end of the rain. Nadine couldn't be much longer. But hang about, there was a man opening the side gate. That would be her co-host. Jack jumped out of the van, closed up and hailed him.

'Hi there!'

The man was a short, elderly man with a grizzled beard, wearing a black beanie in spite of the warm weather, baggy trousers and a mauve over-washed t-shirt.

'Can I help you?' said the man.

'Yes,' said Jack. 'I said I'd help Nadine today. She's delayed.'

'What's going on over there?' He pointed out the house. 'All those cops and people in white crime gear.'

The man had undone the padlock and swung the door inside.

'There's been a murder,' said Jack. 'I'm working there. Well, I was. It's a crime scene now. Nadine's being questioned. She'll be over soon.'

The man beckoned him in. Jack went through the door, which the man put on a hook in the open position.

'Who's dead?' he said.

Jack wondered whether to tell him. It couldn't be much of a secret. Everyone in the house knew. It would be out soon enough, but not for him to mouth off.

'Better not say,' he said. Playing safe. He'd talked too much already.

'If it's not Nadine,' said the man, 'well, I doubt it's her husband or her daughter... Or she wouldn't come in today.

I'd guess Mo. I know he deals, and got some dodgy acquaintances. So yeh, Mo.'

'I'm not saying,' said Jack, though impressed with the analysis.

'Can I put a bet on it?'

'No.'

He smiled and put his hand out. 'I'm Howard. I do Thursday afternoons. Nadine's not usually Thursdays, but it's holiday time.'

Murder time, thought Jack.

'I'm Jack,' he said. 'A builder held up by murder.'

'Is that your van over there, Jack of All Trades?'

'That's me.'

'I've seen it around the streets. Always gives me a laugh that Jack of All Trades logo. You must do a lot of local work.' Howard glanced at his watch. 'Let's open the front gate.'

Jack followed him into the garden, through the raised beds constructed from thick wooden beams. Railway sleepers, thought Jack, or maybe old church timbers. They continued by the locked container and under a roofed walkway. Howard stopped.

'That water barrel is full.' He pointed it out. 'How come? There hasn't been enough rain to fill it. Nowhere near enough.'

Jack said nothing.

Howard went to another barrel.

'This one is full too. Some kind water sprite has been filling our barrels.'

Jack kept his counsel and followed him to the front gate. Howard might not think the sprite so kind if he knew the cost of the water. He opened the two padlocks with his keys and swung the wide gate.

'We are open to the world.'

A man jumped out of a van parked outside. Jack knew him at once, brown overalls, curly hair. And he knew Jack, or rather he thought he did.

'A letter for you, Mr Nick Baldwin.' He handed Jack a letter. 'I wouldn't delay in responding if I were you.'

He turned about and went back to his van, getting in and slamming the door. Missive delivered, he was quickly away.

Howard stared at Jack. 'You're not Nick Baldwin. He's Nadine's brother in law.'

'I'm not.'

'Why did he think you were?'

Jack didn't reply for a few seconds, wondering whether to come clean or add to his lies. Except Howard had seen the water board man deliver the letter, and mistake his identity.

'It's complicated,' he said, scratching his neck. 'Don't know where to start.'

'I'm not going anywhere.'

Jack put the letter in his back pocket. He had decided, muddled as it was, to say nothing more on the matter. He'd only just met Howard, and had no idea whether he'd be helpful or makes things worse for him.

'That letter is addressed to Nick Baldwin,' said Howard.

'I'll give it to him,' said Jack.

'But he thought you were Nick...'

'I was working with Nick,' said Jack. 'He got our names mixed up. I'll give him the letter. Don't worry.'

Chapter 22

Nadine was in her sitting room, seated in an armchair. A strange situation for her, as the two cops had taken it over. An Asian guy and a tall white woman. She was uncomfortable in their presence, never quite trusting the police. She wondered how much Jack had told them.

'You are Nadine Baldwin,' said Hayley, looking at her notes. 'Wife of Ace Baldwin and mother of Sally Baldwin.'

'I am.'

Easy so far. Wouldn't stay that way, she knew. You wonder about people like her. How many wrongful convictions had she been involved in? Keep the arrests coming in. Up the stats. They stick together, her lot. A club of liars.

Take care.

'Who else is living in the house?'

'There's my mother-in-law, Marta Baldwin. She's lived here a number of years. And Nick Baldwin, who is Ace and Mo's brother. He's just staying for the time being.'

'Why is he staying?'

'He's got personal problems.'

'Can you tell us more?' said Hayley.

'I'd rather not. You'd best ask him.' She shuffled in the seat. It was hot. They hadn't opened a window. Her room, but she didn't feel she could do it herself. No way though was she going to set them nosing into Nick's business. She suspected it wasn't all above board tax-wise.

'Your daughter is having some difficulties.'

'Some.' Nadine shrugged. Why did they have to know everything? All this fishing.

'She's not at school today.'

'It's almost the end of the school year,' said Nadine. 'They're not doing anything. So hardly matters if she's there or here.'

'She's pregnant, isn't she?'

'Why is that important?'

'We don't know what's important at this stage,' said Hayley. 'But she is pregnant and we believe Mo had some involvement.'

'Why do you believe that?'

'It's better if I ask the questions, Mrs Baldwin.'

Nadine stood up. 'I am too stressed out for this inquisition. I don't have to put up with it. Do I?'

'It's either here or at the station,' said Hayley.

'Am I a suspect?'

'Everyone is a suspect, Mrs Baldwin.'

'Please don't call me Mrs Baldwin.'

'Why not?' said Hayley. 'Isn't that your name?'

'Enough, enough.' Nadine held her hands before her like a fence. 'I will come to the police station later. But I won't answer any more questions here. In my own sitting room.'

'If you don't come to the station today,' said Fayyad, the first words he'd uttered during the interview, 'we will charge you with obstruction of justice.'

'Then you'll beat me up, and plant evidence,' she said. 'I know the way you guys operate.'

She strode out of the room, slamming the door behind her. Hayley and Fayyad let her footsteps echo in the hallway, as they took in their dismissal. The police constable entered.

'Any trouble there, sir?'

'A difficult customer,' said Fayyad. 'We've invited her to the station later.'

'Shall I bring down the next?'

'Give us ten minutes. In fact...' He took out his wallet. 'There's a cafe round the corner, will you get us some teas? Milk, no sugar, both of us. Get one for yourself.'

The constable took the bank note.

'Thank you, sir. I know the place. Forest Cafe. Just a few minutes away.'

He left them.

Fayyad stood up and stretched.

'Bit stuffy in here. I think we'll open a window.'

He went to the window, unhooked the clasp and opened the window. He came back and sat on the arm of the sofa. Hayley had risen and was stretching her arms wide.

'What did you make of Mrs Baldwin?' said Fayyad.

'She certainly doesn't like cops.'

'Thin skinned. Like we were touching an open wound. I didn't think your questions were especially challenging.'

'Well, I'm a white woman, she's a black woman. I've come across that reaction before. They don't trust us. Some history in the family.'

'I'm sure that's part of it,' mused Fayyad. 'Lots of prejudice involved in stop and search. A constant gripe.'

'Saves lives,' she said.

'Maybe.' He shrugged. 'Definitely creates resentment though. And non co-operation. She wasn't going to tell us anything about anybody.'

'We told her more than she told us,' said Hayley with half a laugh. 'Which makes me think she has a fair bit to hide.'

'Like murder?'

'She was shifty. Wanted to get away like she was in a house on fire. I don't think it was simply dislike of cops.'

Chapter 23

Howard suggested that Jack might clean out a couple of bird boxes. If he didn't mind. Jack was amenable, now he was here, and waiting for Nadine. He was itching to look at the letter, suspecting it was a demand for lots of money for taking water illegally. But had no opportunity, not with Howard here. And having said he'd give the letter to Nick.

'The boxes have been occupied by blue tits and the nestlings have fledged,' said Howard. 'Can get mucky in there with parasites and such, so wear gloves. And put the debris in a plastic bag and bin it.'

Jack had taken down two nest boxes. One had been on a tree trunk, the other on the fence. He put them on a large wooden cable reel, now in use as a table. As instructed, he wore gloves. Jack was curious what he might find inside.

Forget the letter. Things had just happened more quickly than he'd hoped. Look at it when you leave. The worst it can say is Nick Baldwin owes the water board lots of money. Jack had a thought, and half grinned to himself. Might be an idea to give it to Nick. He'd just chuck it on his pile of unpaid bills, and it wouldn't be burning a hole in Jack's pocket.

Yeh, give it to Nick. And act dumb.

The bird boxes were wooden, with a circular entrance, the size of a golf ball. From the first, he pulled out a couple of nails, and a side came off. Inside was a tangled, tight nest made of moss and grass. There were bits of eggshell and some fluffy feathers stuck in it. Jack pulled the nesting material out and a couple of earwigs scurried across the nest box floor. He looked at the nest mass, now on the table. A tight bundle, there could be anything in it, tiny bugs and who knows what. He dropped it into a plastic bag and tied the top securely.

He opened up the second. It was much the same, but dustier, with tiny mites scurrying about. Straight in a plastic bag, tipping in as much of the dust and mites as a few taps would allow.

Jack binned the nest debris and filled a bucket from a water barrel. Collecting soap and scrubbing brush from the shipping container, the source of all tools and gear, he began scrubbing the inside of the boxes, thinking, as he did so, that they were getting a better clean up than his kitchen.

But that was the way of it. After a job, he'd hoover and sweep the way he rarely did at home. Not that he had parasites and creepy crawlies. He hoped.

There were a few other visitors in the garden. A young woman was walking around with a toddler stumbling along beside her. That top heavy age with a big head and small feet. Howard was talking to a couple by a wildflower bed, or at least that was what Jack had been told the bed was. It was colourful, he had to admit, and even recognised a few plants to his own surprise. Red poppies and some dandelion-type flowers, a group of giant daisies, but nothing else. The rest was a jumble with bees and butterflies flying between.

Nadine came in, while Jack was scrubbing out the bird boxes. She hadn't seen him and was looking around, searching. Then spotted him and headed straight across. He could see by her face, something had vexed her, and she hadn't yet seen the water board letter in his back pocket. Give it to Nick. Get rid of it.

But she was riled, without him adding to it. That was clear.

'What did you tell the police?' she hissed.

This was war mode. He recognised it from his ex. Hands on hips, waiting for the wrong answer.

'The truth,' he said.

'Don't you know they twist everything?'

'I didn't tell them anything they wouldn't find out anyway.'

'How do you know?' she said sharply.

'Everyone in the house knows Mo was Sally's dealer. One of his pals got her pregnant...'

'And you came straight out with it, like a snitch.' She shook her fists. 'Oh, you white people, the police on your side... There's a crime, they see a black person. Guilty!'

'I don't think it's going to be like that.'

'You don't know anything. My cousin died in police custody. The way they manhandled him in the station... There was an inquiry. And they got a reprimand. And that's it. A black man's dead. And a few slaps on the wrist for the cops that did it.'

She sank onto a nearby seat. Jack didn't know what to say. He was 'white people' now. Yes, he was wary of cops but couldn't compete with her tale. There must be another side, but on no account must he voice that.

He said, 'There's been a murder, Nadine. They have to investigate it. How can they if they don't ask questions?'

Her face had sunk into her hands, elbows on knees. She didn't speak for half a minute. Jack scrubbed the inside of the bird box. Soap and water, suds, scrub out the dirt.

Without looking up, she said, 'I walked out of the interview. They knew Mo was dealing, knew Sally was pregnant. You were first in line. You told them.'

He didn't say anything. It was hardly a question, more an accusation.

'I have to go to the police station and make a statement,' she said, 'or I could be arrested for obstructing justice.'

Jack doubted they would. But then he was 'white people', so maybe they would.

'I let him in,' she said.

'Who?'

She looked up, her face bleak.

'Mo. Last night.'

It hit him. So this was it. Walking out of her interview, thinking the police were about to fit her up. And she had cause, rightly or wrongly.

'Why did you let him in?'

She bit her lip, obviously deciding whether to tell the snitch. But then she'd already opened the box.

'Mo tapped on my downstairs window,' she said, 'about 11.30 last night. I was doing some bookkeeping. I opened the window a little. We had a brief chat. I wasn't going to let him into my flat, though that was what he wanted. To sleep on my sofa. No way. I told him he could sleep in the garden shed. I got my sleeping bag, went out my door, and gave it to him. Then I opened the side door, and let him in. And that was that.'

'You didn't follow him in?'

'I told him to sleep in the shed. Left him there. Locked up. And went back to my flat. That's all.'

'Why couldn't you tell the police that?'

She sighed and shook her head. 'You ask me that, Jack. After I've told you about my cousin...'

He said, 'They're already wondering who has a back door key.'

'Just me and Ace.'

'So Ace will know it was you.'

'But the cops won't.'

He could of course tell them. And no doubt she was thinking just that.

'What do you think I should do?'

Jack thought, what would he do in the same situation? What might the cops think?

What should a black woman do?

He said, 'Go back and tell them. Don't let them catch you out lying.'

'I haven't lied,' she said, 'just not said.'

'If you don't tell them...'

'You will.' She challenged him directly.

'No, I won't. But if you don't tell them, when they find out, they'll arrest you.'

'I can't allow that. Not with this job, with Sally pregnant...' She scratched her hair, and growled like a cornered animal. Then rose. 'You are talking sense. Sorry I had a go at you.'

She crossed to him and gave him a brief kiss on the cheek. And then was away. He watched her walking away across the garden. She went to Howard, who was cutting back a shrub. They talked briefly. Then she left him.

And was out the side gate.

Chapter 24

'What was your relationship with Mo?' said Fayyad.

Nick was in the armchair before the two cops. They had already discussed his bankruptcy, his wife leaving him. Hard opening your soul to the fuzz. The woman cop was scribbling a lot as he spoke. The sleeves of his grubby shirt were rolled up. Clearly he hadn't washed in a while, and was smelly in the heat.

'Didn't have much to do with Mo the last year or so,' said Nick. 'I don't live here normally. Just been here the last couple of days because of my troubles. Mo used to try and catch me in one of my shops, and ask for money. When I stopped giving him any, he stopped coming.'

'Did he have enemies?'

Nick smiled. 'Drug dealers always have enemies.'

'What about in the family?'

'Well, Ace hated his guts.'

'Why?'

'He doesn't like scroungers. Thinks everyone should make their way in the world like he did. And of course there's Sally. You know about Sally?'

'What do you know about Sally?'

Nick laughed.

'She's Ace's daughter. Mo was selling her stuff. And getting her in trouble, and introducing her to unsavoury characters...' He stopped. 'I shouldn't be saying all this. Telling tales. I'm sure you know already.'

'There's been a murder, Nick. And it's quite likely someone in the family did it.'

'I'm a suspect? Am I?' He tapped himself on the chest.

'Everyone in this house is.'

'Even the builder?'

'Let's press on,' said Fayyad. 'You were telling me why Ace didn't like Mo. His scrounging, and his relationship with Sally? Were they intimate?'

'Don't think so. But you never know with Mo. He'd sleep with a dead dog, so I doubt his niece would be off limits. But I never heard.'

'The baby isn't his?'

'So you know about that. Well, well. Someone's been telling tales ahead of me. The baby...' He gave a short laugh. 'Who's the daddy? I don't think it's Mo, but what do I know? I mean, I never expected Sally to be expelled. Posh school out in Essex. And then it comes out she's expelled for dealing, and pregnant too. Nothing would surprise me now.'

'Mo was selling her drugs?'

'So I am told, and leading her astray. But I really don't know much about this. It's all second hand stuff to me. Sally hasn't told me anything. It's only what I've picked up from the others. Ace gave us chapter and verse last night in the sitting room. What a bombshell! He made it clear, oh did he, that Mo was persona non grata in this house. No one must let him in. As for Sally, well, we mustn't let her out. But I tell you, I'm hardly in the know about what she's been up to. All been news to me, her shenanigans.' He shrugged and bit his thumbnail. 'There's something I've got to say though. Been thinking about it for the last hour, and it's no good holding back.'

'Do tell us, Nick.'

Hayley was poised with her pen, waiting. Nick composed himself. He had decided.

'I'm not sleeping well,' he said. 'It's the heat, but mostly my troubles, the bankruptcy and my wife leaving. You know, that stuff I told you about. No point going to bed early and tossing about. So I was watching TV about midnight, drinking tea, eating biscuits. I am going to get as fat as a walrus. That's what worry does for you. Anyway, I heard the front door close. Pretty quiet. I just caught it. So I went to the window, and there was Ace leaving. He went to his car and drove off.'

'Any idea where he went?'

'No idea. All I can tell you is, he came back about two. Crept in quiet as can be. But I was listening out for him. Surprised he was so long. He didn't go straight upstairs but went into the kitchen.'

'How long was he in the kitchen?'

'Quarter of an hour maybe.'

'Could he have gone out the kitchen door onto the patio?'

'Could have.' Nick shrugged. 'Nothing to stop him. He has an occasional smoke, not allowed in the house. So maybe went out for a fag.'

'But you can't say for sure?'

'No. Except it's not too comfortable in the kitchen with the builder here. The table's gone. There's a few chairs. Personally, if I'd have made myself say a sandwich and a cup of tea, or whatever, I'd have taken them out onto the patio.'

Fayyad looked down at his notebook, contemplating the new information.

'You any questions, Hayley?'

'None.'

'Thank you, Nick,' said Fayyad. 'We may have more questions later, and you'll need to go to the police station today or tomorrow to make a full statement. But that will do for now.'

Nick rose and said, 'I talk too much. That's what my wife always says. Nick, you should learn to shut up.'

He left them. The constable put his head round the door.

'Next?'

'Give us five minutes, Ben.'

'Right.'

The constable closed the door.

'What did you make of Nick Baldwin?' said Fayyad.

'We could do with some air freshener,' she said wrinkling her nose.

'Definitely depressed. Washing and shaving not on his agenda.'

'Or clean clothes.'

'What do you make of that about Ace in the kitchen?'

'For quarter of an hour,' said Hayley. 'Plenty of time to go out on the patio and stab Mo.'

'Certainly. Ace is well in the frame. But where had he been for two hours?'

'Sex or drugs or rock'n'roll?'

'I doubt it was to do his accounts,' said Fayyad.

Chapter 25

Mia had caught a bus from Ilford where she'd been shopping. Her school was in Stratford, so no way would she shop there on her day off. Someone might spot her. Ilford was far enough away. She'd not seen anyone she knew, and had had a pleasant day, spending the £300 given her by Sally on a phone and tablet. Great spending someone else's money. But she felt she had to get value, as Sally was paying her two hundred. Though when she did a count up in a toilet, she found she'd lost forty. How had that happened?

That annoyed her. A lot of money for her, forty quid. Nothing she could do, though. Could have dropped it anywhere. Still, that left enough. After she'd bought the gear, she thought of going to a cafe to eat, but she was wearing school uniform and felt conspicuous. So Mia went to a delicatessen and bought olives, salad, cream cheese and beigels with orange juice. She went to Valentine's Park, where she was fine for fifteen minutes until plagued by two sixteen year old boys obviously bunking off. They were beginning to get rough, so she ran off, afraid they might take the tablet and phone in her bag. And her own phone too, without her having any way to complain, not with dodgy money involved.

She got free of them, having to leave half her lunch behind. They could have that, and good riddance. Now she had to drop off the booty in the community garden as arranged. Either Sally would be there or, if she wasn't, Mia was to hide them under the container-cum-tool-shed.

Nearly there. Offload the gear, and she'd have done her dirty work.

The time for them to meet was 1pm. That was if Sally could persuade her mother to let her go to the garden. It was only across the road from her house, and Nadine might be working in the garden, so Sally had thought it likely.

Mia hoped Sally would come as she hadn't spoken to anyone all morning. Apart from those louts in the park, and that was hardly a conversation. In her backpack, she had a sponge cake and bananas she'd bought when she got off the bus. They could share. Sally had said she'd bring some picnic stuff too. She hoped that she had some drink. It was hot, sticky weather. She'd have a shower when she got to Dad's after the drop off.

Mia entered the garden via the side door and looked for Sally across the vista of raised beds, trees and shrubs. She couldn't see her, but that didn't mean she wasn't here. There were plenty of hidden spaces: front, back, in the greenhouse, on the staging. If Sally wasn't here, that would be a pity, but she knew what to do: tuck the gear under the container. And then go to Dad's. He and she could have the cake when he got home. A surprise. If he got back early, she'd need to make up a reason for being there. Easy enough. School was so lax these end-of-term days.

No one really cared whether she was in or not.

There was a huge buddleia at one end of the garden, with high, bending boughs of leaves and purple flowers, going up twelve feet or more. A jungle. She recognised it as they'd done a project on the plant. Buddleias grew just about everywhere, once you started looking, you could see them on waste land, up walls, on rooftops even. They had been brought over from China in the 1890s and escaped from gardens. Some people hated it. Mia liked it; buddleia was a sort of rebel, an escapee, making the best of things.

Oh heavens! there was Dad. She dived into the thick of the buddleia. What on earth was he doing here? She peered through the branches. He was supposed to be working in the house opposite, not cleaning bird boxes. Cleaning wasn't his thing anyway.

She still hadn't seen Sally. Mia glanced at her phone. It was 12.55, so she was a little early. She'd wait for twenty minutes. Dad was busy, he'd never spot her in here. She thought of leaving, then coming back in quarter of an hour. That risked being seen as she left her hide-away. Best stay here where she could keep an eye on him.

If Sally didn't come, how would she get the gear under the container without being seen? There was no way she could contact Sally who was of course without a phone.

Worry about that later.

*

Jack took his gloves off. He had finished cleaning the bird boxes. The refuse had been dumped. Nearly there. Just let the box pieces dry in the sun, then re-assemble. Half an hour should be plenty, then put them back together, and get them back up. Job done. A little task, but surprisingly satisfying; he smiled at his pleasure, not exactly building work, taking out a couple of nails, but he'd made a clean home for the next residents, come the spring.

Not all his work was so valuable. Take a contested kitchen island, as an isolated example.

Jack was seated at the reel table, eating a sandwich, when the man came. He was thin, short, in a t-shirt with a rock band motif that Jack had never heard of, torn jeans, and wearing a Harry Potter mask, Afro hair just showing above it. He had a leather bag at his waist, hanging by a long strap round his neck.

Seeing Jack, he crossed to him, rocking slightly on his feet.

'Where's Sally?' he said through the mouth of the mask. A broken tooth was just visible.

'Sally who?'

'Don't mess me around, I want Sally.'

Why was he wearing a mask? What was in his bag? The man was wearing black kid gloves. Every signal told Jack to be wary of this aggressive guy. The rocking motion and a sweetish, acrid smell, skunk was it? He'd taken it once at a party. It had made him ultra paranoid, figuring everyone there was in a conspiracy against him. Not a drug this guy needed.

'I don't know where she is,' he said, held almost in a trance by the Harry Potter mask fixed on him.

'So you do know a Sally?'

'But I don't know where she is.'

The man was twitchy, looking about him as if Sally might suddenly appear. He turned back to Jack. And in one swift movement, he pulled a revolver from his bag.

'Get in there!'

He indicated the container with a gloved hand.

Jack jerked in shock. He was four feet from a gun barrel, aimed at his chest, hardly missing distance, stoned or not, six bullets in the cylinder. He could see the tips of them. The man was serious. And to prove it, he cocked the hammer.

'I don't know where she is,' he repeated helplessly. 'Sorry.'

But he did know where she was. In the house, grounded. He wasn't going to say that to a man in a mask with a gun. And just hoped that was sensible of him.

'One last time, fella. Or I'll blow your head off. Get in there.'

The man pointed to the container with his free hand, the other holding the gun, aimed squarely, if a little shakily, at him. Jack was alert, heart thrashing, aware of every motion of the man. The mask, the gloves, the gun barrel, the command. Do nothing to disturb the guy. A simple squeeze of the trigger and Jack would be a goner. He walked obediently to the container, stepped over the ledge, and stopped, just over the threshold, and glanced behind.

'Get inside. Further in, right down the back.'

Jack walked through the boxes and sacks, into the gloom, to the shelving at the back containing cans of paint. The only light was that coming through one half of a double door, the other not open.

'Stay there, face the wall,' ordered the man. 'Move and you are sprayed chicken.'

Clear enough. Jack stayed at the rear of the container, his back to the door, arms obediently by his side. To his front were cans of paint, brushes and adhesive in deep shadow. He didn't know what the man was up to, or even where he was, but could hear him calling. Was he going to be shot in here? Why? The man wanted Sally. She had certainly met some unsavoury characters through Uncle Mo.

This had to be one of them.

Jack considered making a run for it, but had no idea where the man was. It would take him several seconds just to get down the length of the container. Too late anyway, as he was aware of other people coming in, shadows moving across the shelves in front of him. Who, how many, he couldn't tell. Several.

'In, right in,' the man yelled, 'or who wants to be first to get a bullet?'

Jack could hear them entering, stomping towards him. Shadows crossing and recrossing the paint cans.

'Back, back, right back.'

They stumbled further in, until they were with Jack by the shelves of paint. Jack glimpsed Howard to one side, as the gunman began to close the container door. The light was shutting down, shadow eating colour, and in a few seconds, with a clang of metal on metal, they were in complete darkness.

Jack turned around, away from the shelves. He could see nothing in the pitch black. He heard a lock click, then another. They were totally sealed.

'Don't panic,' he said, to people he couldn't see but whose breathing he could hear. 'We're safe in here.'

Not that Jack was much below panic level himself. A loaded gun on you sure speeds the heartbeat. He turned on his phone, so he could see by its light. There was Howard, with a young man and woman, and a toddler.

'He's closed the padlocks,' Jack went on, 'I heard the clicks. But he hasn't got the key to re-open them. He can't shoot through steel. We're safe in here. Just relax.' Adding a second later. 'If you can.'

He was telling himself as well as them. Take it easy. Though, he was still in flight mode. There was a masked man with a gun out there. He'd locked them in, but could no longer get to them.

Howard switched on his phone light.

'Somewhere back here is a battery light,' he said fumbling through boxes. 'I hope it's charged. One of those jobs you mean to get round to. Not important most days, as you don't plan for being held up and locked in.'

He groped around in the half light. 'Somewhere on this shelf, in this box, I think. Got it!'

Howard was holding a black box with a bulb behind glass at one end. He switched it on. The light was dazzling, appearing brighter as they'd been in the semi-darkness a while.

'It's still got half its charge. That's maybe 90 minutes.'

The young man said, 'That Harry Potter mask gave me the shivers. As much as the gun.'

'My daughter has one,' said Jack. 'A mask I mean, not a gun. But it's not her,' he added in an attempt at levity.

No one laughed. Shaken out of everyday life, adrenaline flooded, they were attempting to reorganise the world, in a compound of fear, reason and unreason.

'I've no signal on my phone,' said the woman. 'Has anyone?'

They looked at their phones. None of them had a signal.

'What are we going to do?' she said.

Not the most comfortable of places to make a strategy. They were hemmed in by shelves, tools and gear in cardboard boxes. Half of it junk probably, he thought. He knew from his own lock-up how it piled up. At least, they had light and company.

'We've got biscuits, drinking water, cups too,' said Howard, going through a box, 'and enough air for, I'd say, two days.'

'That's not funny,' said the woman. 'Not with Harry Potter outside waving a gun.'

'Sorry,' he said, 'but we can still have biscuits.'

'I don't want biscuits,' she said raising her voice. 'I just want to get out of here. Alive.'

The young man put his arm round her. The child had found a child's trowel with a smiley frog face on the handle, and took it to his parents. Mummy took it, and the child went back for another. He'd found a box full.

Lucky kid.

Jack said, 'Give it half an hour. For the gunman to go. Then we attack the door with a sledgehammer. There's one hanging there.' He pointed it out. 'If we make just a small gap, that should give us a phone signal. And we can call the cops.'

Howard arranged some crates for them to sit on in a circle, clearing away sacks and cardboard boxes to give them leg room. He placed an upturned crate in the centre, as a table. On it, he put two packets of biscuits: custard creams and digestives. From the shelving, he brought out plastic cups and a litre of water, and began the picnic, taking biscuits and water for himself. He offered them around.

Like a Jewish mother. In a crisis. Eat, family, eat.

The young man declined a biscuit, suggesting they introduce themselves. Adrenaline was subsiding, pulses getting closer to normal. The young man began, giving his name, their street, and what they did on earth. And round the circle.

They were safe, here on the boxes, the child playing with the frog trowels. There was a man outside with a gun, but in their cave, they had all they needed.

'Like Jonah,' said Howard. 'We're in the belly of a whale.'

'He didn't have a light or biscuits,' said the young man.

'He had God,' said the woman.

'Didn't God get him thrown overboard in the first place?' said Jack, trying to recall his Sunday school lessons.

'No,' said the woman with finality.

He wasn't going to argue. She seemed to know, and Jonah was hardly relevant to their present predicament. He munched a digestive, swallowed a little water. This was like camp. They just needed song books and a fire. Not such a good idea; the smoke would choke them.

Give it half an hour, and then he'd attack the door.

The woman had the toddler on her knee. The little boy was munching a custard cream. She began singing:

> *The wheels on the bus go round and round,*
> *round and round,*
> *round and round.*
> *The wheels on the bus go round and round,*
> *all day long.*

Chapter 26

Mia stayed still in the buddleia. She was laid out flat, not daring to move, the branches towering above her, ants scampering in the soil, white butterflies flittering through the leaves. She couldn't believe what was happening. Here in the garden. It was like a horror film. A man, wearing a Harry Potter mask with a gun, had forced her dad into the container and then other people. He'd locked them in. And probably would have put her in if he'd have seen her.

There must be plenty of air inside. They'll be alright, she thought. They weren't packed in, and had light from their phones. Could they phone the police? Might not be a signal. She dared not phone herself as she was too close. The man was yelling at Sally, who'd come in at the wrong moment. Mia could hear some of what he was saying to her. Something about an abortion, or not an abortion, and she was yelling back. Stupid of her, he's got a gun. Calm him down, Sally. Agree with everything. Don't shout at him.

Mia had a phone and tablet in her backpack, the ones she'd bought for Sally. And there was Sally as arranged. But there was the masked man with a gun, not part of the arrangement. He'd closed the front gate and the side gate, so no one else could come in. Mia was trapped along with everyone else. Except Harry Potter didn't know she was here.

She'd felt so free in the morning, doing her shopping in Ilford. Out of school, getting a good deal on the items. Her picnic in the park would have been great, if those louts hadn't come. And here was another one.

Worse even.

What made people so aggressive? Some of the girls at school could be pretty belligerent. It was said a couple of them had knives, but this guy was waving around a loaded revolver. He'd taken off his mask. He was maybe a white guy, maybe mixed race. Was his hair curly or Afro curly? She'd be rubbish in a line up. Mia attempted a photo of him with her own phone. Through these leaves, it'd be useless. She took a couple more.

The man slapped Sally, and screeched at her:

'You filthy, selfish bitch. You do what I tell you!'

She'd better, thought Mia. Don't argue with him. Please. Just do what he says, agree with everything he says.

He pushed Sally into a chair. The one where her dad had been sitting ten minutes ago. He laid the gun on the table, within easy reach. Taking a scarf from his bag, he tied it round her mouth. And then drew out handcuffs. Mia couldn't quite make out through the buddleia jungle what he was doing with them. Then a click, and glimpse; they were on her wrists.

Here, in the garden, in broad daylight. Her dad and the others locked in the container, and she hiding, in fear of her life. It was like being in a movie, except no one was going to shout, 'Cut!' And she doubted the gun was full of blanks.

Mia was shivering in spite of the heat. This is what happens when you bunk off school, she could imagine her mother telling her. If her mother ever would. Mia was the only one the gunman didn't know about. The one still free, if this could be considered any sort of freedom. Her legs were quivering as if she'd run a mile.

A little way behind her, in the middle of the buddleia, was a small shed. The children's book shed, she'd looked in once when she came here with her mum a couple of weeks

130

back. It had lots of picture books on low shelves, a children's stool, and posters on the walls about all the millions of plastic bottles that we throw away, and the 6th great extinction. A bit much, she'd thought at the time, for picture book kids. But aim high, as her teacher said.

Mia took off her backpack. She'd be quieter without it, less encumbered. She tried to still her breathing. Her legs hardly belonged to her, they were like creatures attached to her body, untrained, loath to do what she wanted. She was barely in control, terror at the wheel. It would be easy to surrender, to cry out: *I'm here*, and end the tension one way or another.

The man was putting a hessian sack over Sally's head. He was talking to her softly, Mia couldn't make out any words, nor would they have made any sense if she could hear them. Mia inched backwards. Slowly, slowly, on her belly, backwards, until she could no longer see the man and Sally through the foliage.

The fear had all but numbed her. As if she were on a sheer mountain face, unable to climb up or down because of the thousand foot drop below. A single look down would cause giddiness to unbind her grip on the rock and she would fall, down, down, into the void.

Slowly, inch by inch. Don't cry, don't yell, inch by inch. That's all you have to do. Inch by inch. Her shoe scraped the wood of the shed door...

There was a fierce bang. Her stomach leapt. Must be a shot. She hoped it was a frightener. It certainly scared her soppy, if there was any higher level for her fear to climb. Another shot, as she opened the door of the book shed. Inch by inch; it creaked as she eased it wider. She lay still and prayed she hadn't been heard. The man was speaking but she couldn't make out the words. He seemed less angry, now he had Sally hooded, gagged and handcuffed.

She must be alive, if he was talking to her. Mustn't she?

Poor Sally.

She couldn't hear her, just the man. Had he shot her? Wounded her perhaps. Or firing shots to keep her terrified. He had taken the mask off, she'd noted in her earlier glimpses. Sally seemed to know him. Oh pray, he hadn't shot her. Let Sally be alive.

Mia was in the shed, hunched on the kid's stool, as if she were of picture book age, pulling the door slowly shut. Why hadn't they oiled it? The ear-splitting creak... She held her breath and waited, crossing her fingers. She was far enough away, surely, and he was too occupied to hear the door.

Or he could be just out there, set to rip the door wide and reveal her crouching.

Breathe slowly. Mia took out her phone. Her fingers thick as if cold with frost, clumsily striking the buttons.

She could hear it ringing. Please, please, don't be difficult. She pressed it hard to her ear, turning down the volume.

'Police, fire or ambulance. Which service do you require?'

'Police. It's an emergency.'

She waited, aeons, aware of the hissing in her ear. Had they forgotten her?

'This is the police. How can we help you?'

'There's a man with a gun in Forest Gate Community Garden,' she said in a hushed voice, hearing the words as if they were coming from another speaker. 'On Earlham Grove. I'm in there, hiding. Please come. He's locked people in the container. He's got Sally Baldwin gagged and handcuffed. He might have shot her. I've heard a couple of shots. Please come at once.'

Chapter 27

'I know Ace,' said Hayley to Fayyad. 'We're in the same martial arts club.'

They were set up to question Ace, in the downstairs sitting room.

'I've only ever seen you in your judogi,' said Ace. 'You look strange in civvies.'

'Ditto.' She turned to Fayyad on the sofa. 'We're both black belts. We've fought even.'

'Who won?'

'I did,' said Ace, adding quickly, 'But she's good.'

'Not quite as good as you, it seems,' said Fayyad, noting that Ace was keen to admit his superiority, but allowing that she was good. A good mannered sport.

'Enough sports chat,' he went on. 'And as you two know each other, it's best that I take the interview. I am Detective Sergeant Fayyad Kamani, this is Detective Constable Hayley Amis who you know. And you are Ace Baldwin.'

'I am.'

'This is an informal interview, Ace. May I call you Ace?' Ace nodded. 'Fine. We will need a formal, recorded statement at the station. Which you can do today or tomorrow, but no later than tomorrow, please. The sooner the better, while events are fresh in the mind.'

'I understand. I'll go this afternoon.'

'Good.'

A window was open and a fan had been brought in, but seemed to be just blowing the heat around. On the table was a jug of water and some plastic cups. The bin underneath was filling up with paper and cups.

Ace was in a well-cut, sky blue suit. He'd undone the jacket buttons on account of the heat, but the formality of the occasion stated he should keep it on, along with his red tie. On this, possibly not much else, he and Fayyad were in agreement. The man had standards. And looked after himself. He was heavy, but muscular, certainly not fat. And he had floored Hayley, whom Fayyad had seen in action. So impressive.

He glanced at his notes.

'What's your relationship with Nadine Baldwin?' he said.

'We are man and wife.'

'She has told us that she is applying for a divorce.'

'I don't believe in divorce. A man and woman marry for life. No ifs, no buts.'

'This is her flat though, this basement?'

'In a manner of speaking. I own the house, so in truth it is mine. She has taken the flat over while we are estranged. It was rather a fait accompli. Her studio had been down here for some time. She paints. This sitting room was my weight training room. While I was in Birmingham for a few days on business, she moved all the weights, bench and stands to the bedroom upstairs. Set up her bedroom down here, bought a new bed even. I came home, and here she was. In. Like a squatter.'

'That's quite a heavy description, Ace.'

'The house is in my name, clearly. We are husband and wife. I do not agree with divorce as I've said.'

'Therefore she's not a squatter. If she's your wife.'

'That's her opinion too. But she can't have it both ways.'

Fayyad was puzzled. Was Ace referring to the basement flat or the divorce? Hayley nudged him. He took the point; he was going off piste. Ace's thoughts on divorce and ownership might be confusing, but were marginal to the case in hand.

'We'll leave that,' he said. 'Tell me about your relationship with your brother, Mo.'

'It's no secret, I didn't like him. And everything I've learnt about him since, has proved me correct. He was a wastrel, a drug dealer, and heaven knows who his friends are.' He stopped for a second and corrected himself. 'Who his friends were. One of whom got my daughter pregnant. When I found out last night, about his disgraceful goings on, I kicked him out.'

'Someone let him back in.'

'It wasn't me, I assure you.'

'You went out late last night, Ace.' Fayyad looked at his notes. 'From about midnight to 2 am...'

His phone on the table rang.

'Excuse me, but I need to take this, it's operational.'

Fayyad listened, his body stiffening as the call went on. Hayley and Ace just hearing Fayyad saying yes and OK a few times. He closed the call.

'We must terminate this interview, Ace. I am sorry if that is an inconvenience. But there's an incident in the community garden opposite. An armed response team is going in, and DC Amis and myself are required on site.'

Chapter 28

'Let's get started,' said Jack.

He was impressed with the range of tools and equipment in the garden container. Howard had found him gloves, goggles and a helmet. Jack had at first thought he might be able to use a cold chisel and club hammer. But there was no gap between the doors to get the chisel in. He'd just have to bash the doors and make one. Brute force, to make a smallish space, in the hope that would be enough for a phone signal.

'Stand well back, everyone.'

Jack glanced behind to make sure he had plenty of room, and then swung the sledgehammer at the door with full force. It struck with a ringing crash, the container reverberating beneath their feet, bits and pieces trembling on the shelves. The force of it jerked back through his body almost knocking Jack over.

'If he's still out there, he must have heard that,' exclaimed the young man.

'But he can't do anything, George,' said the woman. 'We're locked in and he hasn't a key. That is so, isn't it, Jack?'

'It is. Besides, I am not out to smash the door in. We just need a gap so we can phone the law.'

The man mumbled something incoherently. His wife put an arm round his shoulders and he gripped her waist. The toddler was placing the froggy trowels carefully back in the cardboard box as Jack swung again. The container rocked; a box of dried-out felt tip pens fell off a shelf.

Howard picked them up and pushed them further in. Jack examined where he had struck. There was a bulge but as yet no gap where the edges of the doors overlapped.

It was tiring, just a couple of hits, not so much the strike itself but the recoil through his body. He hoped his joints could take it. But needs must. Jack struck again. The recoil was instant, jarring through his arms and body, but the note of impact was different.

There had been give. And yes, there was a chink of light.

'Look!'

He indicated a glowing hole. Tiny, but oh so there. The others came forward to see this minuscule gateway to the outside.

It occurred to Jack, this would make a perfect pinhole camera. There'd been an article on their use a few months back in his astronomy mag. The thought of being inside one was quite overpowering. Even if out of place.

Some other time. Or maybe not.

'Turn off the light, Howard,' he called, 'and your phones, everyone.'

They did so, not understanding what he was up to. Jack stood back from the pinhole of light, and gently moved everyone else back. There was a very faint pattern of the buddleia jungle, upside down, on the others' faces. But it didn't really work, too much stuff in here. You'd need a white screen in the right place...

Jack forced himself back to the matter in hand. When would he ever be inside a pinhole camera again? What an idiot! He took up the cold chisel and club hammer, doubting the others would be interested in his obsession. Concentrate. Who knows what is going on out there? Get the police here. ASAP.

There was a hole he could work on and widen, hope-fully enough to get a phone signal. A bit more bashing, then try the phone. Jack put the chisel end in the hole and gave the head a couple of hard knocks with a club hammer.

'Stop hammering!' came a voice from outside. 'We know you are in there. We're going to open up. Put the hammer down please.'

'That's my mate!' Jack exclaimed to the others. 'It's the law!' He put his mouth to the hole and yelled. 'Tools are down. Waiting on you.'

'Opening up, right now, Jack, and whoever else is with you.'

'It's Fayyad,' he said to the others. 'I know that voice well enough. A local cop. A friend. Must be OK out there. Harry Potter has gone.'

'Thank goodness,' exclaimed the woman. 'We just came to the garden for a picnic... My Facebook group won't believe a word of this. I don't myself.'

Jack removed his gloves, helmet and goggles as the padlocks were being undone. They waited impatiently for their rescuers, all looking to the door, Jack gazing at the weak image the pinhole made on their faces and boxes of light. Needs a screen in the right place, he thought. Too diffuse now.

He gave up his chaotic thoughts. The outside world was coming in. Soon the Facebook telegraph would be pinging with tales and pictures. Who was out there, besides Fayyad? How had they known to come? He glanced back at the others, strangers who'd become almost a family for half an hour. United by a masked gunman.

The door swung open. For a few seconds, all he could make out was a silhouette that he knew to be Nadine against the blinding sunlight. He stepped outside, blinking rapidly, the shapes beginning to fill in without colour and features.

Flooded with relief as well as with light. The cavalry had come.

There was Fayyad and Hayley with Nadine, watching them all as they stepped out, one by one, from the container, and into the safe world. Not quite so, there were armed police with automatic rifles in the garden. One watching them, rifle at the ready, just in case any of them were armed. Others were searching the buddleia. And there was Mia. What was she doing here?

She ran to him.

'He shot Sally!' she exclaimed. Her face was smudged with dirt and tears.

An armed policeman called out, 'Follow me to the rear of the garden, please. That area is clear. The gunman may still be around. This way, please.'

All followed, apart from those armed police whose mission was to scour the end of the garden they were leaving. Jack took a glance back. The blue line was slow and thorough, going through the buddleia, looking behind and under raised beds.

Mia was by his side holding his arm. It hardly seemed the same garden that they'd been forced out of. He looked at his watch, forty minutes had passed. Trees, shrubs, flowers should have been shattered wrecks in the mud and trenches, and yet here they all were, greeting him.

What was it Mia had said about Sally? A look at Nadine's face, heavy and tear ridden, told him of a tragedy. Shot, but was she dead? There was no sign of medics. He was reticent to ask.

The group were halted by the pond, where a pair of blue damselflies hovered over yellow flowers, oblivious of the danger at the other end of the garden. Bees were buzzing around at the water edge.

'Please stay here,' said the armed policeman. 'You're safe. Don't go down that end until we give you permission.' He indicated the area out of bounds with his rifle, the sceptre of absolute authority.

There was a bench alongside the pond which the man, woman and child claimed. Howard brought over a few plastic chairs for the others. A uniformed policeman was despatched to bring tea.

'Are you all OK?' said Hayley, inspecting the former prisoners for signs of stress. 'Do any of you require medical attention?'

'We're fine now,' said the woman. 'Howard gave us water and biscuits in the container. He found a light too. Quite cosy, in a way. Oh...' She suddenly remembered. 'Our picnic bag is over there.' She pointed to where.

'We'll get it for you in a few minutes,' said Hayley. 'Don't worry about it.'

'How did you know we were in there?' said Jack.

'Mia,' said Hayley, looking to the girl. 'You tell them.'

'I was hiding in the buddleia,' said Mia. 'I crawled into the kids' shed and phoned the police.'

'Oh you saint, you wonderful girl,' exclaimed the woman. She swung round to address her rescuers. 'It was glorious when you guys opened up. All the light hitting us. Like Dorothy coming out of her house in the Wizard of Oz.'

'Is Sally dead?' said Jack to Fayyad, a sentence he wanted to retract as a glance at Nadine's tearful face gave him the answer.

'She is,' said Fayyad.

'He put her head in a sack,' exclaimed Mia, unable to stop her burbling. 'There's a big hole in it, going into her brain, blood and bits of bone everywhere.' She shuddered, her eyes welling. 'It's horrible.'

Jack put his arm round her. What was Mia doing in the garden at all? This was no time to ask her. Besides which, she had phoned the police, for which he was forever grateful.

Nadine was seated on the other side of Jack, trying not to weep, but not succeeding.

'I am so sorry, Nadine,' he said, words inadequate. What can one say on such occasions when the worst has already happened?

'Thank you, Jack.' She wiped her eyes with a tissue. 'I don't know the half of what my daughter was up to, who she'd been meeting. But why kill her?'

'He was stoned,' said Jack. 'Out of his head, no sense of consequences.'

Fayyad came over.

'Mia,' he said. 'You have been awfully brave. I know it's been terrible, but we'd like to ask you a few questions. Your dad can be with you. Are you OK with that?'

She nodded. 'Yes, I am.'

Fayyad took them a little way from the others. There was a raised wooden stage, about a foot high. On it there was a round, weathered table and few chairs. They seated themselves as the constable returned with the teas in a cardboard box.

They were given a tea each, and Fayyad allowed them to settle.

'You're not in any sort of trouble, Mia,' he said, 'you have been heroic. But we need to know what's been going on in order to catch the killer. And you saw more than anyone else. So please tell us what you witnessed. Your dad won't let me pressure you. Just a few questions to help us, Mia. For a start, today is a school day, so why were you in the garden?'

She looked around at her dad and the two police officers.

'You're not in trouble,' said Jack. 'You're safe, that's all that matters.'

'I bunked off school,' she said.

'I don't care.'

'Tell us why you were here,' said Fayyad. 'Slow as you like.'

Mia hesitated, took a gulp of tea and began.

'Sally gave me money to buy her a tablet and phone. I bunked off school, as I said.' She glanced guiltily at her father.

'No matter,' said Jack, with a dismissive hand.

'I bought them in Ilford,' she went on, 'and was due to meet Sally here at 1 pm. But I saw Dad, at the table, where Sally is now...' She stopped for a few seconds, tears welling. Hayley handed her a tissue. She dabbed her eyes. 'Thank you.'

'Your father was here,' prompted Fayyad.

'Yes,' she said. 'Dad was here, cleaning out a bird box. Sally hadn't come then. I hid in the buddleia, so Dad wouldn't see me. I should have been at school. Anyway, I wasn't. And I hid in the buddleia. Then the man came in wearing a Harry Potter mask. I saw him stick Dad up with a gun, and make him go into the container, and then he rounded the others up. He had a revolver, like they have in cowboy pictures. He pushed everyone into the container. Then he locked the doors on them. And put the padlocks on.'

Mia took a sip of tea. Fayyad, Hayley and Jack waited on her. Her tale, in her time.

'I was lying in the buddleia all the time,' she went on, 'flat out, not daring to move as I knew if I did, he'd shoot me. He'd have to, now that he'd locked the others in the container. He wouldn't undo it just for me.'

Jack knew the man couldn't undo the padlocks as he didn't have the keys, but didn't interrupt her flow.

'Then Sally came. She was there to meet me. I told you that. I was going to give her the tablet and phone. I've still got them, here, in my backpack. Do you want to see them?'

'That's not necessary,' said Fayyad. 'What did you see the gunman do? When Sally came.'

'He was shouting at her, she was having a go back at him. He took off his mask, he was a white guy or maybe mixed race. Yelling about an abortion. I couldn't catch the sense of it. But like he knew her. Whether he wanted her to have one or not. I'm not sure what he wanted. Do you think he's the father of her baby?'

'Could well be,' said Fayyad. 'Let's be clear, Mia. I don't care about you bunking off school and buying gear for Sally. That's not a police matter. Though your dad might have something to say.'

'I'm just glad she's safe,' said Jack.

'Don't tell Mum.'

'I won't,' he said, knowing that was a lie as the story was bound to come out. It'd be on the news. There'd be an inquest some time. Mia was the main witness. But he'd choose his time. And likely, as the sun comes up in the morning, Alison would blame him. He'd had no idea Mia hadn't gone to school. Though it was through him that Mia had met Sally.

Something occurred to him.

'Did you lose forty quid?' he said.

'Yes. Did you find it?'

'I did,' said Jack. 'On the carpet at home.'

'Do I get it back?'

'That's to be discussed.' He'd spent some of it, on an unhealthy lunch.

She nodded.

'Carry on, Mia,' said Fayyad, 'when the gunman was with Sally. What else did he do?'

'He kept yelling at her for a while,' said Mia. 'And, as he had his mask off, I took a few photos. I reckoned as he was watching her, he wouldn't spot me. I don't know if they are any good as it was through the buddleia leaves and branches. I just snapped away on my phone. Do you want to see them?'

'Most definitely. Carry on.'

'There's not much more I can say. I didn't see her get shot, I just heard it. I'd sneaked backwards to the kids' book shed. I was inside. I couldn't see anything. The buddleia is all over it anyway. I crouched down, there's a little stool in the shed. And I phoned you lot. There were two shots, but I didn't know what was happening. I just kept small and waited, hoping the man wouldn't come looking. I nearly died when the door opened. And there was a man pointing a rifle at me. I didn't see he was in uniform. I could just see the gun. 'Don't shoot, don't shoot,' I called, my hands over my face. He said, 'We're police, love. You can come out.' And he put down the gun, and helped me out.'

Chapter 29

After Mia had transferred her photos to Fayyad's phone, Jack and his daughter were told they could leave. By that time, the garden had been gone through by the armed response team, and there was no sign of the gunman.

'If you don't mind, Jack,' said Fayyad, 'I'll call round this evening. Say 9 o'clock. Just to mull things over.'

'Fine,' he said. That was a world away.

Jack said goodbye to Nadine, saying he'd call her in the evening. He would have hugged her but there were too many people milling. A few lame words was all. Nothing that could mitigate her sorrow. Not that that was possible. He imagined how he would feel if it had been Mia. And it could have been, if she'd been found by the gunman. He'd be inconsolable till the stars went cold.

Back home, Jack made tea. More tea. The lubricator in difficult times. Something warm to hold, though their flat was stuffy with summer heat. Jack opened the sitting room window. Mia sat on the sofa, Jack at the table.

'Show me the cash and gear,' he said. 'The lot.'

From her backpack, she took out the tablet and phone, and scrunched up banknotes from her pockets. She laid them out on the table.

'The phone is new,' she said. 'The tablet is second hand.'

'How much money is there?'

'Well, I had lunch and fares out of it. And you've got forty. Here's a receipt for the phone, and here's one for the tablet.' She handed them over. Jack glanced at them. They were receipts from Ilford shops. 'The two come to almost £285 in total,' she went on. 'I've got some coins too...'

'Forget them.'

'In notes...' Mia went through the fluff of notes, sorting them into piles of fives, tens and twenties. She counted them. 'That's £155. And you've got forty. All that's left of 500 pounds.'

'She gave you all that!' Jack whistled. 'Where did she get it from?'

Mia didn't speak for a little while, playing with crumbs on the table. Then said. 'Guess.'

'Proceeds of drug dealing,' he said. Mia nodded. 'She was expelled from school, she told me. Quite a business woman. Way out of her depth.' He felt around in his pocket. 'I haven't got all the forty. I spent most of a fiver on lunch.' He placed thirty five pounds on the table with some change.

'Forget the coins,' said Mia, with the hint of a smile.

Jack retracted the change.

'One hundred and ninety quid left over,' said Mia. 'We're not going to give it to the police, are we?'

Jack considered it. Alison would hand it over without question. Well, she was a head teacher. A moral guardian. He was less a virtuous defender. If Mia wasn't here, he'd simply pocket the cash. But she was, and he was a parent, and supposed to be a role model. Heaven help him.

'The police don't have to know,' added Mia helpfully. 'The school didn't call the cops, so they won't know Sally had the money.'

'How much more did she have?'

'Another few hundred. Under a floorboard in her room.'

'The police will find that for sure,' said Jack. 'They'll do a thorough search of her room.'

'They won't know it's drugs money,' she said.

Or care, thought Jack, not with a murder taking centre stage. They'll put it down to a schoolgirl hiding her savings.

'Put the money, phone and tablet in the drawer,' he said. 'So we are not distracted.'

Mia reluctantly opened a sideboard drawer.

'There's money in it already,' she declared, holding up a twenty pound note.

The three hundred he'd put there this morning. Several lifetimes ago.

'Leave that,' he said. 'It's work money. Put yours in the drawer next to it.'

Mia found an old envelope on the sideboard top. On it, she wrote the date and £190, amusing Jack that she was keeping tabs on it. She stuffed the money in the envelope and put it in the drawer with the phone and tablet.

No honour among thieves, he thought.

They showered in turns, and had more tea, some toast, the old standby. Mia played some keyboard, tried reading but was somewhat listless. Jack searched through his old astronomy magazines. And found what he was looking for: the article on the pinhole camera in a feature on watching an eclipse of the sun safely. The author suggested using a cardboard box, such as a shoebox, as a pinhole camera. No mention of shipping containers.

He considered writing to the editor, but dismissed it, as why he was in the container would be too complicated to explain. Besides which, it had barely worked. Though the hole was still there in the door. He could put a sheet screen up, and it might give a better image.

Nadine would not be interested. In pinhole cameras or anything else. Some other time, weeks hence maybe. She was grieving. He'd talk to her this evening, though quite what he'd say he was unsure.

Around 7 pm, they went to see Alison in hospital. Jack had bought flowers, which wasn't too smart, as she had a florist of blooms. Fellow teachers had come from her school bringing bunches which overwhelmed theirs.

She was sitting up, quite cheerful, reading a novel.

'It's so nice to have time to read a good book,' she said. 'I should break my leg more often.'

'It's not *Catcher in the Rye*,' said Mia.

'Didn't fancy it. It's a Nicci French. They're a couple, you know. Great crime writing.'

'How was the operation?' said Jack.

'Better than I thought it was going to be,' she said. 'Local anaesthetic. I couldn't see what they were doing as I was lying flat out while they put a plate in my right leg. Didn't feel a thing. Took about an hour, I suppose. I'm sore in the calf what with stitches and all, but OK. How was your day?'

Jack told her about Mo's murder where he was working. That kept her wide eyed. And was fairly safe ground.

'You do get into some scrapes, Jack,' she said. 'And how was your day, Mia?'

'Boring,' she said. 'Just playing games and watching a film.'

'What film did you see?'

'We watched *The Tempest* with Helen Mirren. It was good, the only part of the day that wasn't a yawn.'

Jack was impressed at Mia's capacity for untruth. A teenage gene perhaps.

Chapter 30

Fayyad phoned to check Jack was in, and came over. They left Mia doing Facebook stuff in the sitting room and went into the kitchen.

Jack put the kettle on.

'What were the photos like?' he said.

'One was good,' said Fayyad, seated at the kitchen table. Jack had cleared it, knowing he would be receiving a visitor. 'And we have fingerprints too, even though he was wearing gloves. On the handcuffs.'

'Careless of him,' said Jack. 'But he was quite stoned.'

'One especially good print. And it was on our database. Not surprisingly, the man has quite a record. Dealing drugs, robbery with violence, burglary. His name is Kingsley Dayville. We are certain of it, as Mia's photo matches his mugshot. So no doubt at all.'

'Any idea where he is?'

'No. He obviously fled the community garden before we'd got there. Turns out, he climbed over the back fence into an Asian family's yard. He threatened them with a gun, still wearing his Harry Potter mask. They were only too pleased to let him out of their yard. There's a full alert out on him. I'm sure we'll pick him up pretty soon.'

'Let's hope so, he's dangerous. Do you think he's the father of Sally's child?'

'Quite likely. We'll do a DNA match with the foetus. We have his on record. If Dayville has a fifty percent match with the foetus, then he's the dad. It'll be a few days before we know. There's always a queue on DNA testing.' Fayyad sighed. 'The post mortem is tomorrow. Me or Hayley will go; I hate those things. The smell of formaldehyde and all the cutting up of flesh. The pathologists are so matter of fact. It's like a slab of meat to them. They tell jokes, talk about their weekend at the seaside.' He shivered. 'While I'm trying hard not to vomit.' He shrugged. 'Part of the job.'

'How did Sally choose such a lowlife?'

Fayyad shrugged. 'Teenagers. What do they know? Your daughter excluded.'

Jack wouldn't exclude her, but wasn't about to tell a cop about Mia accepting Sally's drugs money.

'It's most likely,' went on Fayyad, 'that she met Kingsley at a dive called the Shindig. Mo, her uncle would you believe it, took her there. It's in our sights. Drugs, probably guns, who knows what else?'

'Why don't you shut it down?'

'Drug squad.' He shrugged. 'A law unto themselves. I don't know what they're up to half the time. They sometimes let a place run, so they can keep an eye on it.'

'Not impressed,' said Jack. 'We have Sally dead. Mo dead. Uncle and niece. Mo introduced her to Dayville, father of her baby, most likely. At the Shindig, which the drug squad are supposedly keeping an eye on.'

'Are the two killings connected?' mused Fayyad.

'Surely,' said Jack mulling it over as he poured the tea into their mugs. He'd put out a plate of biscuits, left over from a pack they'd collected from Alison's the other day. He was pleased with the addendum. Up a grade on his usual hospitality.

'Did Nadine come back to talk to you?' he said.

'She did. She'd walked out of the first interview. Said that you persuaded her that wasn't a good idea. She apologised for walking out. Said it was stress. It's obvious she doesn't like cops.'

'She had a cousin die in custody.'

'That would explain things.' He half laughed. 'I get it from both ends, Jack. Sometimes I'm Uncle Tom, being a cop at all. And it's not worth explaining that I'm not that sort of black. But sometimes, I'm Asian, and I can get info others can't. It's a fine line, race. Words change their meaning... I'm less sensitive these days. Which I'm not sure is a good thing. I tend to let things go. You can't keep challenging people.'

'Nadine let Mo in last night, didn't she?'

'She told us. Around 11.30. Through the side gate and into the garden. She gave him a sleeping bag, so he could sleep in the shed. And that was that, as far as she is concerned. According to her.'

'Is she a suspect?'

'Of course she is. She had no choice but to tell us she had let him in. We'd already reckoned Mo most likely came in via the garden door. And only she and Ace had keys. So one of them let him in, and it was unlikely to be the man who had kicked him out.'

'You're improving. Might make a detective yet.'

'Thanks for nothing.' He took a custard cream. 'Here's another line for you to contemplate. Ace was out somewhere, so Nick tells us. No love lost between those two. Anyway, Nick said he was watching TV in the sitting room and saw Ace leave around midnight.'

'Any idea where he went?'

'No. Ace's interview was interrupted by the events in the community garden. We're going to continue the interview tomorrow. We've got him and his mother to do. Another team are taking the statements from the community garden, your fellow detainees. We'll need yours too, Jack. When you come to the station...' He stopped, with a look of concern at his friend. 'How you bearing up, Jack? It's no joke having a gun pointed at you.'

'A bit shaky. Could've gone bad for us. But once he'd locked us in, we were safe enough. He couldn't re-open the padlocks. Not without the keys. Anyway, it's Sally he was after.' He paused for a second. 'Something has struck me.'

'What's that?'

Jack scratched his head. 'We know why Sally was there. To meet Mia and get the phone and tablet from her. That's clear. But how did Dayville know she'd be there?'

'I've been wondering too.'

'Someone must've told him. File that. Likely to be important.'

'How's Mia?'

'Seems OK, considering. But you never know. She didn't actually see the murder, but saw the build up. And she saw Sally's body.'

'Not a pretty sight.'

'Just have to see how she goes. I'm going to have to tell her mother, Alison, but not just yet as she's in hospital with problems of her own.'

'Will she be out soon?'

'A day or two, on crutches. The sooner the better.' He crunched a custard cream, reminded of the picnic in the container. Safe in the stomach of the whale, while outside a storm raged... Jack took a sip of tea in an effort to evade the image of his daughter watching the gunman and Sally. 'Two murders,' he mused. 'Got to be connected. I keep getting back to that. I mean, other than by Mo introducing Sally to Dayville.'

'I'm pretty sure there's a connection. Two in the same family. Got to be. But how?'

'It centres round Mo,' said Jack. 'He introduced Sally to Dayville in the first place. That lowlife gets her pregnant, kills her for whatever warped stoned reason. No doubt about her killer. But how does that connect to Mo's death?'

'Could Dayville have killed Mo too?'

'Not likely. It can't be ruled out, but I think Mo's death is a family affair.'

'Makes sense,' said Fayyad. 'A lot of tensions and hatreds among the Baldwins.'

'So how do the two killings tie up? They've got to. Same family, less than 24 hours, and 100 yards, apart.' He flapped a hand dismissively. 'We're missing something. More info needed. Down to you guys. And in the meantime, when can I get back to work?'

'I was going to tell you,' said Fayyad. 'CSI have finished with the kitchen. They'll still be out on the patio and back garden tomorrow, and they'll be going through Sally's room. But you can work in the kitchen.'

'Pity the patio is out of commission,' said Jack. 'I'll have to cart bricks through the house. Can't be helped, I suppose. My employer wants me to get going or I'm out on my ear. Today's halt he can hardly blame me for. But tomorrow, I'll have to work like a Trojan.'

Chapter 31

After Fayyad had gone, Jack was concerned for Mia who was listlessly watching a nature programme about orcas and seals in the Shetlands. He watched it for a minute or two. The orcas, aptly known as killer whales, were trapping a seal in deadly teamwork. Jack wondered whether it was appropriate, all considered. It was nature, and nature was cruel, murderous. A comedy or a romance would be more soothing.

The orcas had just got the seal, the sea was turning red...

'Is there nothing else on?' he said.

'Just rubbish.'

Which didn't mean it was rubbish, just that she didn't want to watch it. Nor did he want to have a go at her. The seal was dead and the ripping apart was going on under water. Not exciting enough for the film team, who switched to puffins nesting. Cute little birds. Better.

'I'm going to wash the dishes,' he said.

'That'll be exciting for you.'

'As much excitement as I can take tonight.'

Jack went into the kitchen. The excuse was the dishes, but he felt he should phone Nadine. Duty rather than desire. He'd said he would. Jack filled the washing up bowl with soapy hot water to delay the inevitable.

And he washed the dishes. There wasn't much, just the cups he and Fayyad had used, and their biscuit plates. For once, he was reluctant there weren't more. He'd run out of displacement activity.

Nothing for it. Jack wiped his hands, sat at the table in hesitation mode for five minutes. And dialled.

'Hello, Jack.'

She sounded distant, as if on a rock out at sea.

'Hello, Nadine. What's it like at your place?'

'Like a mortuary. I'm downstairs in my sitting room. I've been watching a programme about orcas surrounding a seal. And I'm thinking about all the killing in the world. War, shootings, knives. Legal, illegal. At least orcas do it for food.'

'Human beings can be awful,' he said.

'What's the point?'

'You mean of life, the Universe and everything?'

'Marta was telling me it was God's plan. I walked out on the stupid woman. Why would any God plan to have a 17-year-old girl murdered?'

'Ask my mother. She'll tell you.'

'She won't know,' said Nadine. 'She'll go on about the mystery, the things we can't comprehend. As if that's any sort of answer to Sally getting a bullet in her head.'

'Have you talked to Ace?'

'He's as cut up as I am. We talked a little, he's religious, don't I know it. But even he couldn't take Marta's simplicity.'

They were silent. He felt the pressure to break it.

'I'm back at work tomorrow,' he said.

'Might see you, if I can get out of bed. I've things to do. That is, things I'm supposed to do. Deadlines. But how on earth can I write a grant application when I feel like death? Everything is meaningless. It's a vale of tears. I'm a wreck.'

Jack was stuck for words. What do you say to someone who has lost a daughter? The usual platitudes. Chin up, time the great healer. Neither would serve.

'I am so sorry,' he said. 'It's awful. There's nothing I can say that's any comfort.'

'Nothing. If you were here,' she said, 'we could cuddle, and I could weep. Wouldn't be much fun for you. So if you'll excuse me, I'll say good night, Jack. I'm out of words, empty as a gourd. The world has lost any meaning. It's all nonsense, keeping ourselves busy so we can't see there's no point to anything.'

And she closed the call.

That had been useless, he thought. He'd wanted to comfort her, but over the phone it was impossible. He didn't know what to say. Was there anything to be said anyway? Nadine was inconsolable. As he would be if it had been Mia who'd been shot.

Jack went into the sitting room.

'Time for bed.'

'OK,' said Mia with a yawn. 'Last day of school tomorrow. Better show my face.'

She went off to wash, and Jack made up a bed on the sofa. This was the routine in his one bedroom flat. She had the bedroom when she was over, he took the sofa.

It was a hot night. Jack found it hard to doze off. The happenings of the day jostled for prominence. Mo's corpse on the patio, a gun in Jack's face in the community garden, being locked in the container, and outside Sally blown to bits. His affair with Nadine had gone backwards, receded into a dim black dot. She was grief-stricken and that left no room for any other emotion.

Mia had had a hard time this afternoon. He hoped she would be OK at school tomorrow. Ideally, he should keep her home, but he had to work to clear his debts. The job had been stop-start, and Ace was cracking the whip. Under-standably, next to nothing had been done. It had to get a move on. Just a small job, three days max. If he could have three days without interruption.

Jack rolled about in the itchy heat. At last, he rose and went to the bathroom. He soaked his face and hair, and the top of his pyjamas, with cool water. There was nothing he could do about anything, not now, this time of night. Why was his mind whirling?

Sleep came somehow, when he'd given up trying.

*

Jack woke in the darkness. Someone was screaming. He lay there a few seconds, as if the cries might have come out of a dream. They hadn't. Mia was screaming.

Jack put on the light, attired himself in his dressing gown and went into the bedroom. Mia was awake, sitting up in bed, hair awry, face pale and strained.

'I've had a nightmare,' she exclaimed. 'Horrible.' She shuddered. 'There was Sally sitting on the edge of my bed, with the bag over her head, and the hole through to her brains. She was telling me the tablet was useless, the phone was junk, and she was going to strangle me for wasting her money. Then she came for me, blood dripping all over the bed as if she was a watering can...'

'I think you'd better get up,' said Jack, cutting short the gruesome description. 'Put on your dressing gown. I'll make us some tea.'

Five minutes later, both were in the kitchen drinking tea. And more biscuits. Too many biscuits today. Definitely not good for him, biscuited up. Fruit and veg, the health mantra. Tomorrow. Definitely tomorrow.

Good food eating would start.

It was twenty past three in the morning, dark outside. He'd put on Radio 2, which at this time of night played easy music for insomniacs and night workers. Mia wasn't going to school tomorrow; he couldn't evade it. She was in no state. With Alison in hospital, he would have to stay home.

No argument.

Not with her at least, but Ace would get shirty.

They played a game of Chinese chequers. She won; he'd planned to let her, but didn't need to as she won anyway. Then Mia had an idea. She got the money from the drawer, the money that Sally had given her, and divided it in two. They played pontoon for it. Jack played outrageously, doubling up to recoup his losses, and again. Until he'd lost the lot.

It made him think of Nick who had been playing for real. Double or quits. And Nick had lost the lot. More than the lot, including the cash he owed Jack and 100 others.

Jack said, 'You're staying home tomorrow. I won't go into work.'

'I could go in,' she said. 'I'm OK.'

'No,' he said, having decided. He'd have to tell Ace what was what. And if Ace sacked him, too bad. 'You're too shaky,' he went on. 'You can't go to school. It's not your fault that there was a murderer in the community garden. Mind you, you shouldn't have been there in the first place, but that's another matter.'

'I called the cops.'

'You did. Which is why you're getting away with it.' He yawned, following up with a groan as he looked at the time. 'Let's try to get some sleep at least, I'm like a zombie.'

'I'm keeping the light on,' she said.

Jack and Mia went back to bed. He hoped for a few hours' shut-eye, though not so important as he wouldn't be working. The pain of the call to Ace in the morning. He'd tell him he wasn't coming in and suffer any sanctions Ace cared to put on him. The worst it could be was losing the work.

He'd survive, one way or another.

Chapter 32

Jack woke around seven thirty, a little later than his usual time, but it didn't matter. He just had to catch Ace, then he could go back to bed. He let Mia sleep on.

He made some tea, had some toast. And a banana. Would that do, diet wise?

At eight, he phoned Ace.

'Hello, Jack. What can I do for you?'

'My daughter isn't too well, after yesterday's happenings. She had an awful nightmare. I'm going to have to stay home with her.'

'What about her mother?' said Ace.

'She's in hospital with broken bones. A car accident. I am sorry,' said Jack. 'I would be in if I could, but she's only a kid, no matter what she thinks she is, and she saw what Dayville was up to.'

'Who's Dayville?'

Of course, Ace wouldn't know that. Fayyad had only told Jack last night.

'Sally's killer. The police have identified him.'

'That's something, I suppose. This is dreadful, Jack. I am just moving around on automatic pilot.'

'My full sympathy,' he said. 'It's dreadful for sure. My daughter was in the garden, she phoned the police. And she saw Sally's body. She seemed fine in the evening, then in the early hours she woke me up screaming.'

'No one should have to see that,' said Ace. 'Certainly not a kid. Dire. I had to identify the body. Awful, awful. No father should have to see such sights.'

'I am so sorry, Ace. A terrible time for you. But Mia too. She never has nightmares, but she can't just throw off what she saw. Like yesterday's shirt.'

'I get it,' said Ace. 'I'm a parent.' He corrected himself, saying deliberately: 'Was a parent.'

'You look after yourself, Ace. I'd be devastated if anything like that happened to Mia.'

'I hardly slept a wink. Such a shock. Mo's death hardly bothered me. He was my brother but I had lost all respect for him, but Sally's death pulled the rug from under me. I've never been hurt so much. Never ever, as in the mortuary, looking at her corpse. The hole in her head. She, utterly lifeless...' He didn't speak for about ten seconds, then more firmly, as if he'd shown too much weakness. 'What is done is done. Let's be practical, if possible. When can I expect you back?'

'Mia's mother will be out of hospital tomorrow. It's Friday now, I could come in Sunday.'

'Come Monday,' said Ace. 'But I can't pay you for the days you're not working.'

'Yes. My hit.'

'I hope your daughter recovers quickly. She's a brave girl from what I heard.'

'Thanks.'

'Bye for now.'

He closed the call.

That wasn't bad, thought Jack. Not Ace's usual dressing down. He'd been quite civilised, sympathetic even. A grieving parent. Well, well, it just goes to show there is some blood in the man.

Jack had another cup of tea and a bowl of muesli. He'd murder for a slice of bacon. You must be able to get used to muesli, he thought. Grains and fruit, so earthy. Alison swore by it. She would, Mia too. One of those sex linked genes then.

A text came.

160

Surprisingly, it was from Nadine:

Sorry I was so unfriendly last night. My death wish. I couldn't see straight or think. Ace has told me you can't come in because Mia is suffering. Why don't you bring her here? Then you can work. I'm just going to do some daubing, not fit for much else myself. Mia can paint too. X Nadine

Well, all change. Nadine would look after Mia. Fine for her, fine for him. Get on the move.

He woke Mia and told her what was happening.

'She's Sally's mother. Isn't she?' she groaned, half asleep.

'She is. Says she's not fit for work, you can do something with her. She's an artist.'

'Sounds OK. Better than being bored round here.'

She rose, washed, had a bowl of muesli and they set off.

Mia was quite chirpy in the open air. She'd woken up, no ghosties on the street. Jack was pleased that they would both get what they wanted out of today.

Arriving at the house, they went down Sally's steps to her basement front door. Jack rang the bell and Nadine opened up.

'I am so glad to have some company today,' she said as they came in. She'd showered, Afro hair tied back, in workaday jeans and t-shirt. 'Thank you so much for coming, Mia. I was dreading being on my own all day. I thought we could do a collage together.'

'Sounds fun.'

In the hallway, Jack said, before leaving them, 'One thing, before I go up top. Sally has some money under a floorboard. A few hundred quid, didn't you say, Mia?'

'Yeh, something like that.'

'Get it straightaway,' said Jack to Nadine. 'The cops are going to search her room today. And they'll have it. Better that you do. Leave a little, just some notes, so they aren't suspicious.'

'Will do. Thanks, Jack. I'll just settle Mia.'

Jack left them and went up the inside stairs. In the hallway, he noted that all Sally's coats had been removed. He guessed it was Marta, as he couldn't imagine Nadine or Ace summoning the energy. And no bike. Vanished from the face of the earth.

In the kitchen was Ace drinking a coffee. He was suited and smart with a dark green tie on a pale green shirt.

'I thought you weren't coming in, Jack.'

'That's how it was forty minutes ago. But Nadine texted me and said she'd look after Mia. So she's downstairs and I can get on with the job.'

'Excellent,' said Ace. 'I'd told Nadine you wouldn't be in. We do talk sometimes. Anyhow, good to see you.' He looked at his watch and sighed. 'I wish the cops would get here. I did half an interview yesterday, and they want to do the rest today. But where on earth are they?'

'They do work very late,' said Jack, recalling Fayyad's visit last night.

'So do I,' said Ace. He was pacing around, his coffee in danger of spilling. 'I must go into work. I can't stay around here. There's either Nick cursing me, or my mother telling me Sally's death is part of God's plan. How can it be if He gave us free will?'

Jack was almost knocked over in the vehemence, as if he had been arguing against him.

'Nothing to do with God,' he said. 'A nasty killer was one hundred per cent responsible.'

He had the vision of Dayville in his mask, holding the gun on him, asking for Sally's whereabouts.

'My feeling exactly. You can't bring God into everything.'

Ace went to the kitchen door, peering along the hallway, and then went out, as if looking would bring the police quicker. Jack got down on his knees and began pressing down the masking tape. CSI had been trampling all over it, scuffing and roughing it up in places. Jack had a reel in his pocket and replaced pieces where they no longer stuck. This was deja vu from yesterday. Though he hoped not to find a body on the patio.

Not that many left in this family anyway. Two gone. Nadine, he knew, was downstairs, and here was Ace. He hadn't seen Marta or Nick. Surely not? He was getting paranoid. Was it really paranoia, with Mo and Sally dead? Not an unrealistic fear to suspect there might be another murder. If it was his place, he'd run around counting who was standing up.

'Crime scene people are here,' said Ace, coming back in. 'So where's the detectives?' He looked at his watch. 'At least in the office, I can get on with things. No one there knows about Mo, or about Sally. And I won't be telling them. Maybe on Monday. The last thing I want is more sympathy. What do you do with it? Bottle it for next year?'

Jack recalled Nadine last night. Nothing he'd said to her had helped. Nor could Ace and Nadine comfort each other. Ace was one of those who worked things out on his own, for good or bad. He'd met the type often enough, worked with them. Admit no weakness. Ace would live and die that way.

He had some of that gene himself. Too secretive, reluctant to ask for help. His drinking days had been a mess of a time, until he'd found Alcohol Halt. Max, his mentor, said don't just look at the negative. That just drags you into a slough of hopelessness. True enough. He was working, Mia was downstairs and seemed fine. A single glance at the family in this house, and how dare he complain about anything?

Jack went to the garden door and looked through the glass to assure himself the patio was out of commission. At least there would be no body out there this morning. Yes, crime scene investigators were there, swaddled in white protective gear. They must've come in the garden door. Already they were at work. One was on his knees on the paving stones, another examining the table. A third was deeper in the garden searching the ground.

'I'll have to come through the hallway with the bricks and mortar,' Jack said to Ace. 'The patio would be easier, but that's a crime scene till who knows when. So I've no choice but to bring the stuff in via the front door.'

'Do what you have to,' said Ace. He was texting, his busy fingers obviously used to the task.

'I'll need to put sheets down first,' said Jack, thinking of the kitchen floor and hall and a full wheelbarrow going in. He'd have to prepare the mortar in here too.

Jack went out of the kitchen, heading for the front door. Going down the hallway, Nick came out of the sitting room.

'Morning,' said Jack, purposely omitting the word 'good'.

'Morning,' mumbled Nick.

Seeing Nick, Jack recalled the letter. He'd utterly buried it in the flow of happenings.

'I've got something for you,' he said. And took the crumpled envelope out of his back pocket. 'Sorry about the state of it, forgot about it with everything else going on.'

Nick took the letter, looked at it in puzzlement, then ripped it open. He glanced at the contents.

'Someone else wanting money. To hell with this.'

He ripped it in half, then again and again, letting the pieces fall on the hall carpet.

'You can't get blood out of a stone,' he said, and went into the kitchen.

Jack watched him go. The letter at least had gone to the person it was addressed to. Not that it solved the problem of the water he'd been involved in stealing. A demand for money. How much, he wondered?

He picked up the pieces of paper, and shuffled through them, trying to make sense of the legal wording in the jigsaw. Ah, there was the figure, £1000, as the man had said, pay up or 'legal proceedings will be instigated.'

Nothing new there. It was as expected, just a little speedier. That tended to be the way when it came to money. Quick to demand, slow to pay.

Jack went outside and along to his van. Nothing he could do about the demand. He certainly wouldn't bother Nadine. He opened the side of the van. Did he have enough sheets? He picked one up and grimaced. It was in a state. An archaeology of twenty past jobs, splattered with paint and plaster, grimy with dust. Jack always meant to wash them after a job, but it was never high on the agenda. Only recalled when the next job was about to start. Like now.

They'd have to do.

Jack pulled out the three sheets and brought them into the house. They'd cover the carpet in the hallway. He'd need newspaper for the kitchen floor. Nadine would likely have some. He went downstairs to her room.

She had a pile of old Guardians.

'I got the money from under the floorboards in Sally's room,' she said.

'How much was there?'

'I got £370. I left four tens, so they'd think that was the money she'd squirrelled away. Teenage savings. I just about got out of the room, when crime scene were coming up to go in. Her room is out of bounds now, they told me. And also said that they've almost finished in the community garden across the road. I'll be glad to see the back of all these cops.'

Here, there and everywhere, thought Jack. But he'd certainly been happy to see them when they opened the container yesterday.

Nadine and Mia were working on a large collage together. It was spread out on the floor. They had 'borrowed' four of his bricks to hold down the thick sheet of paper at the corners. Lots of colour, pictures and text from magazines, fabric, and sections painted in orange and red. Joni Mitchell's *Blue* was playing, the window was open.

It was good to see them both OK.

Jack left them, taking the bundle of newspapers. As he was going up the stairs, he recalled that Nadine didn't know about the demand from the water board. A thousand pounds. Well, she had £370 now, just £630 short. Getting there. Like the church roof fund.

All it needed was a jumble sale and a tombola.

Maybe he should tell her. While she was preoccupied. She wouldn't give a damn about a fine from the water board. Trivial in the scheme of things. Or, then again, she might overreact, her emotions so heated up.

Jack had every excuse not to say anything.

When he got back to the kitchen with the newspapers, Nick was there making toast, having usurped the territory from Ace. It was going to be like this all day, he reckoned. Someone coming in as he worked, and he being the sounding board for their moans, while all he wanted was to get on with the job.

'You know about Sally's death?' said Nick.

'I do.' More than you do, he almost added, laying down the sheets of newspaper.

'Poor kid. But with her parents quarrelling, what do you expect?'

Jack said nothing. He and Alison quarrelled, that hadn't resulted in Mia getting shot. Not as a consequence. Though yesterday was perhaps a near thing.

'They let her run wild,' said Nick. 'Send her to a posh school. But they had no idea what she got up to. Gets expelled, pregnant by a punk named Kingsley Dayville. How's that for a dumb name! While Ace is working all the hours to screw pennies out of blind beggars, then going all out to stop darling daughter having an abortion. While arty wife is downstairs painting and won't be interrupted, and then running over to that garden across the way. Hardly bigger than a sailor's handkerchief. The fuss they make over it.'

There was a screed of complaint; Jack could hardly keep up. He was laying the pages round the perimeter of the island, and out as far as they could be spread.

'Have you ever been over there?' said Jack.

'Won't catch me there. Just a bunch of hippies. I bet they grow weed.'

'I didn't see any.' Then a thought. 'Do you ride a bike?'

'Me? What? Not since I was eleven.' He was wearing the same grubby shirt he'd been wearing yesterday and the day before. 'Why you asking?'

'Thought I saw you, up Plaistow. Night before last.'

He hadn't, of course. It was a try on.

'Wasn't me. I don't go anywhere.'

Jack was on his knees, moving papers about to make the best of them. Was that oil on Nick's turn-up? Something greasy. Didn't have to be oil, he'd been wearing them for days.

'I'm off to bring the bricks in,' he said.

Chapter 33

At Forest Gate police station, the Major Incident Team met at eight o'clock for a briefing on the two murders. They discussed the possibilities that they were connected. The victims were in the same family, the killings were close by and within 24 hours of each other. One was a stabbing and the other a shooting. There was no doubt who had done the shooting, Kingsley Dayville. There were witness statements to that effect, fingerprints, likely DNA corroboration, and even a photo. He was a clumsy assassin who went through a tortuous game with his victim. But the murder on the patio was in another mode, which implied a different killer.

That didn't mean the murders weren't connected, the Chief Inspector pointed out. Keep an open mind, she declared as she closed the meeting.

Hayley and Fayyad set off for the house to complete their interviews. As soon as they were climbing the steps to the open front door, Ace was at them.

'Can we please do my interview?' He was tapping his watch to show how busy he was. 'I have a mid morning deadline.'

'We're going to do your mother first,' said Fayyad.

'Why on earth...!' exclaimed Ace. 'You've done half of mine, and now I am to wait. I shall complain to your senior.'

'Please do so,' said Fayyad. 'Here's my card.'

He handed it over; Ace glanced at the card and reluctantly put it in the top pocket of his jacket. They may well have interviewed him first, but Fayyad didn't like being hassled. It puts you at a disadvantage. You need to show who is in charge.

'Your mother will tell us more about the family,' said Fayyad, 'before we get back to you. Necessary as there have now been two killings. I am sorry if that is inconvenient for you, but murder is rather a nuisance for us all.'

Ace harrumphed, turned about and stormed into the house, to get away from this jumped up cop. He was sure he was being played around.

Fayyad and Hayley came along the hallway and went down the stairs. They settled themselves in Nadine's sitting room. The room was stuffy, smelling of coffee and sweat. Hayley opened a window. Fayyad politely gave the uniformed constable the bin to be emptied, his rudeness expunged on Ace. And he asked for Marta Baldwin to be escorted down.

She entered a few minutes later. Marta was in a black, long dress below her knees and to her neck, with black, flat shoes. A mother, as well as a grandmother, in mourning.

A little tight at the waist and bust, thought Hayley. We thicken as we age, and a mourning dress, not attire worn often, points out bodily change. Unfair, she thought, admonishing herself. The woman had grief enough without her critical thoughts.

'I am sorry for your loss, Mrs Baldwin,' said Hayley after the introductions, attempting to make up for her thought crime. She knew its inadequacy as she said it, but all expressions of sympathy were, in the circumstances. 'I know this is a distressing time for you, Mrs Baldwin, but we need to interview you as early as we can to have a greater chance of apprehending the perpetrators.'

'I cannot believe it,' said Marta, dabbing her eyes with a tissue. 'First one then the other. Why pick on this family? Answer me that.'

'We are here to find the answers, Mrs Baldwin. We know who killed your granddaughter, and we hope to pick him up in the next day or two. All airports and ports have been notified, so he can't leave the country. Police forces up and down the country have been alerted.'

'Bring back the death penalty, I say. Like they have in Jamaica. An eye for an eye, a tooth for a tooth as the good book tells us. Why should that wicked man live?'

'We're the police,' said Hayley. 'We don't set penalties, Mrs Baldwin. That's for Parliament and the courts.'

'He could kill again,' said Marta. 'You mark me well. He knows he cannot be hanged, so after one murder why not make it two or three?'

Hayley didn't point out the flawed reasoning. If he could be hanged for the first murder, then why not go on and kill a street? He only had one neck.

'I understand your distress,' she said, 'but we are not here to argue the rights and wrongs of capital punishment. So, please, madam, let's leave that arena.'

Marta sighed, and set her lips tightly.

'It's Friday today...' began Hayley.

'I lose track,' mumbled Marta. 'One day, another day, all bringing bad news.'

'Where were you, Mrs Baldwin, the night before last, between midnight and two in the morning? That would be Wednesday, going into Thursday early hours.'

'Am I a suspect?' she said affronted.

'Please, answer the question.'

Marta sat up stiffly. 'I was in bed, as every respectable person should be.'

'Did you get up at all?'

'I did not.'

'Did you hear anyone or anything between those hours?'

'I am a sound sleeper. Nothing wakes me.'

'Obviously a clear conscience,' said Hayley. Marta gave a tight smile then quickly culled it as inappropriate. Hayley glanced at her notes. 'Can you tell us about your relationship with your daughter-in-law, Nadine?'

'Nadine and I do not get on,' said Marta. 'She is quite a haughty woman. Over educated, I would say, so she thinks she is better than she is. She is arty, lefty, and she doesn't like the police.'

Marta smiled primly, having offered this pointed characterisation. Hayley held back any comment.

'She arranged an abortion for Sally,' went on Marta, 'which I regard in the same light as hiring a hitman. Thou shalt not kill. That is clear enough in the good book. Once a child is conceived then the child must be born.'

'Did you always get on badly?'

'I have been in this house long enough. Nadine was happy to have my services when Sally was a little girl. I would take her to school, bring her home, make her lunches, and look after her while her mother did her painting and whatever else she did in the community. Her and her committees. Oh, she needed me then. Now she doesn't. And see what has happened.'

'You think she is responsible for Sally's death?'

'Of course. She did not kill her, but she gave up looking after her once she had decided that she wanted a divorce. She ceased to be a wife and mother.'

'Whose idea was it to send Sally to St Anne's?'

'My son, Ace. She couldn't afford it. No way. It is a good Catholic school. But whose fault is it the girl wasn't going?'

Hayley knew Marta's thoughts on that, so took another tack.

'Who do you think killed Mo?'

'I have my own ideas on that matter. Oh yes. Mo disgraced himself. Led Sally into bad company, so she got pregnant, he sold her drugs. Ace had to kick him out. What else could he do?'

'Could Ace have killed him?'

'How dare you ask me that! Ace is a righteous man. He goes to church, he gives to charity. He knows the commandments. He allowed Mo to come into this house, like he was the prodigal son. But Mo took liberties and that gave Ace no choice than to demand he leave. But kill him? Absolutely not.'

'What about Nick?'

'You go from brother to brother. What reason would Nick have? Tell me. I cannot think of a single one.'

'Nadine then.'

'I don't know.' Marta shrugged. 'But I reflect that a woman who can kill a baby in the womb, maybe she could kill a man. I would not put it beyond her, with due respect.'

Chapter 34

Nadine and Mia were having a coffee. Nadine had made up a thermos earlier, so she wouldn't have to go up and down. They were seated on wooden chairs, looking down at the collage on the floor that they had been working on. The window was open, classical music playing quietly.

Nadine was barefoot, which had prompted Mia to take her own shoes off. Both had their hair tied back, and had orange paint on their hands.

'That picture of Sally works well,' said Mia.

'I often do a collage when I'm upset. It's my way of expressing my feelings. Usually, it's not much good, but that's not the point of it. It isn't for anyone else.'

'Like a journal,' said Mia.

'Exactly. Just for me. Not anything you can sell.' She stopped and thought for a moment. 'I'd like you to tell me something, Mia. If you don't mind.'

'Of course,' said Mia, unsure with such an open-ended question coming whether she would mind. But she liked Nadine. This was a comfortable room. And although Nadine was a much better artist than Mia, she hadn't criticised her at all.

'The other night was the only time you met Sally?' inquired Nadine.

'Yes.' Mia nodded. 'I came with Dad. He had to talk to your husband, so Sally took me up to her room and we had a chat.'

'What about?'

'What had happened to her. She told me she was grounded. I asked her why, and she just told me. In fact, I thought she was quite boastful. About being pregnant and being expelled. Like it made her somebody.'

'And you didn't think it did?'

'I thought she was dumb,' she said, wondering as she said it whether she was overstepping the mark. 'Sorry, I shouldn't have said that.'

'No, it's fine, Mia. My daughter was absolutely dumb. I was at that age, but I grew out of it.'

'Dealing at school is crazy,' said Mia. 'You are bound to get caught. The girls get stoned; I know what they'd be like at my school. They'd shop their grandmothers in that state. Then she was bunking off and going to that club, what was it? The Shindig. With her uncle.' Mia reflected. 'Maybe it wasn't all her fault...'

'It wasn't. Mo was twice her age. He had no right taking her there. Or selling her weed.' Nadine sniffed, her eyes welling. 'Sorry. I cry so easily. All the time.'

'It's OK,' said Mia. 'Crying means you care.'

'You are very sensible, Mia.'

'Not so sensible. In fact, I am dumb too. I bunked off school with the money Sally gave me. I went shopping up Ilford. Usually I'd go to Stratford, but that's near my school, Sarah Bonnell.' She sighed. 'It was sort of us, me and Sally, against the grown ups. You know? Like student wizards versus muggles. Sally was grounded, so I was on her side.'

'And the money didn't come into it?'

Mia shrugged uncomfortably and bit her lip.

'Easy money,' said Mia. 'All I had to do was some shopping. And I'd help a girl in trouble with her parents. Ticked all the boxes for me. Tablet – tick. Phone – tick. Great to see what's on the shelves, with lots of money in my pocket – tick tick tick. All good fun. Once the shopping was done, I just had to take the stuff to the garden. No problem. Except there, the story went wrong. Oh so wrong. In the garden is a masked man with a gun, putting Sally in handcuffs and blowing her brains out...'

Mia broke down, setting Nadine off. She put an arm round Mia.

'Poor girl, poor girl. None of it was your fault, love. He was gunning for my daughter. I am sure of it.'

'I'm pretty sure he was the father of her baby,' Mia managed to say through sniffs, leaning into Nadine's shoulder.

'So do I. Kingsley Dayville, she said, was the father. So if that was the gunman... I expect the police will tell me, but then you never know with cops.'

They were silent a while, Mia wiped her eyes and face. They separated, drank coffee.

Mia said, 'Killing a girl because you don't want her to have an abortion... Doesn't make sense.'

'I don't get it either,' said Nadine. 'He's killing his child when he kills her.'

Mia snapped her fingers.

'Maybe he thought she'd already had one!' She shook her hands excitedly. 'That's what she was telling him. It makes sense now.'

'But it wasn't true.'

'No, it wasn't. But she didn't think he'd shoot her. She was lying to take control. She told him she'd already had an abortion. And he shot her for it.'

'Oh, my poor Sally.'

It was Mia's turn to put her arm round Nadine, as they leaned into each other, like two ships after a storm limping into port.

'Oh, what a sad pair we are,' said Nadine through her tears. 'Let's carry on with the collage. Maybe an hour. Not talk so much. Then we can have lunch. Invite your dad down to eat with us.'

'Make it salad and stuff,' said Mia. 'Cut back on the carbs for him. He won't like it. But do it anyway.'

Chapter 35

Jack had made a dozen journeys into the kitchen with buckets of bricks. He'd considered using his wheelbarrow, but getting it up the front door steps would be one heck of an effort. Buckets of bricks were heavy though. So he took breaks, but outside, so Marta and Nick wouldn't see him sitting around, and complain to Ace.

Enough bricks after his back and forth, five in a bucket, until he had a heap of bricks on the newspaper in the kitchen.

Jack laid out the sheet of plastic over the island perimeter, and cut it over size. He'd trim it later. This was the base to protect the floorboards from chemical damage from bricks and mortar. Then he laid bricks lengthwise around the perimeter of the island.

Eager to get laying, this job had been delayed so long, Jack made up the mortar in a bucket. About two thirds of a bucketful, adding water carefully, he stirred the mix with the trowel. The consistency of the mortar had to be just right. Like a firm dough. So it would stay on the trowel to be slapped in the frog of the brick, but still had flow.

Jack got going with the bricklaying. There was no point sticking the bricks to the floor. The island's own weight would hold it in place, especially with a heavy marble top. He went round the bricks he'd laid out, buttering the small edge of each brick, so there was a vertical line of mortar between the bricks in the first layer.

Then, filling the frogs on one long side of the island, Jack began the next course of bricks. He worked slowly and steadily, plying his spirit level every so often. Nick came in, and later Marta, but he wasn't to be distracted and gave short answers to any questions. His concentration caused them to leave him alone.

Jack wasn't a bricklayer; he did some bricklaying from time to time. With just long enough between times for him to forget what he'd learned last time round. Fortunately, this was basic, a single thickness wall all the way round. The trick, perhaps the only trick, was to keep it level as you built a course.

In a couple of hours, he had four courses of bricks all the way round. The island was going to be twelve high. At this rate, he'd finish some time tomorrow. Jack hadn't asked Ace when the marble top was coming. But there was painting to do of the kitchen doors and windows, so if the top was delayed, he'd just get on with that.

Colours for the paintwork, and what was the budget? All the happenings had addled his brain. They hadn't settled on a rate for today. Jack assumed his spying on Nadine was no longer required. Ace hadn't asked for further details about the blonde woman Jack had invented. Hardly important to Ace, when he'd just lost his daughter. Might come up again, but easy to lie and tell him, she hadn't come again, Nadine not being in the mood for any liaisons.

Including himself, as well as his work of fiction.

Halfway round the fifth course, Jack had run out of bricks. He needed to bring in more. It looked good though. The spirit level said flat all the way round. And OK vertically too.

Jack went through the hallway and outside with the bucket. The sun was shining, the heat had built up over the morning. He could do with a cool off, a break. His first thought was to take in some bricks and make a coffee, when he saw a van drive off, one used by the forensic team. Of course, they were working, not just out on the patio here, but in the community garden too, looking for clues on Sally's murder.

He left the bucket at the door, and crossed the road to the main gate of the garden. The wide, double gate was locked. It had a poster on it advertising a summer festival in a week. CSI were using the side gate, but observation holes had been cut in the main gate. Through one, Jack could see operatives stripping off, becoming human once again, as they took off hoods, masks and the white suits.

They were leaving. That was obvious enough.

Jack ran round to the side gate which was slightly ajar. He poked his head in.

'You guys finished in here?'

'All done,' said a man, no longer zombified. 'You can come in if you want. We're off.'

Jack went warily into the garden.

Chapter 36

Ace sat in the armchair before Fayyad and Hayley, glancing obviously at his watch, while Fayyad scribbled some notes. A jug of water with plastic cups was on the coffee table between them. The fan had been turned on and was gently whirring.

'Sorry for the delay, Ace,' said Fayyad, putting his pad down. 'But things have to be done in the right order.'

A meaningless statement, he knew. But Ace didn't know what his mother had said. Nothing particularly revealing, but it did catch the tenor of the family. Who disliked whom the most.

'Yesterday,' Fayyad continued, 'before the interruption, you told us about your relationship with Nadine. About her wanting a divorce and you being totally against it.'

'A man and a woman marry for life.'

'You also told us about your attitude towards Mo. Your antipathy towards him and his lifestyle. Made all the worse when you found out he was your daughter's dealer, and taking her to that clandestine dive, the Shindig.'

'I have no good feelings for my brother. I won't pretend for you.'

'You hated him.'

'Yes.' Ace slapped the table. 'He was a wastrel. I hated Mo. I kicked him out the house. Goodbye, good riddance. I would never have had him back. He could sleep in the gutter for all I cared.' He stopped a second, reflecting. 'You should not speak ill of the dead, I am well aware of that, but I cannot pretend.'

'Your hatred is clear enough,' said Fayyad. 'And understandable, given the circumstances. Sufficient, though, to kill him?'

'I didn't kill Mo. I never wanted to see him again. But kill him? That's not in my nature. I am a man of peace. But I cannot always love my neighbour.'

'Or your brother.'

'Or my brother. But I would not stab him.'

Fayyad looked at his notes in puzzlement. He shouldn't write so quickly, he could barely make it out. Ah yes, got it.

'You were out, the night before last, between midnight and 2 am. Where did you go?'

Ace took a sip of water, and wiped his lips with a tissue.

'To remind you,' said Fayyad. 'That was the night Mo was killed. We know it occurred between the hours of midnight and 2.30 am. And for two of those hours, you were out. Where did you go?'

'I drove around,' he said. 'I went nowhere in particular. I was angry with Mo, that's no secret, and very angry with my daughter for her disgraceful behaviour. How she had been deceiving us! There was no way I could sleep. So I went for a drive.'

'Two hours is a long time to drive around.'

'I drove out to Epping, further, I hardly knew where I was. I had to use my satnav to find my way back.'

'Have you heard of ANPR, Ace?'

'I don't know what that is.'

'It stands for automatic number plate recognition. There are cameras on main roads, and with a number of cameras catching a vehicle, they enable us to tell which route a car has taken. We could use it to find out where you were going, as frankly, I don't believe you just drove around for two hours.'

'I did. It is the truth.'

'As I have said, I don't believe you. If we have to check your movements with ANPR,' said Fayyad, 'we would need to arrest you. For the murder of your brother. That would be embarrassing for you, to say the least. Both at home and at work. The media would pick it up. There'd be cameras out there.' Fayyad pointed in the direction of the street.

'I did not murder my brother. I drove around. I had a head full of worries.'

'Yes, yes,' said Fayyad in exasperation. 'For two hours, round and round, all over the shop...' He stopped and stared at Ace for a few seconds. 'Before I caution you, and take you to the station under arrest, there is another way, which may or may not assist your tale. Let's go out to your car, Ace. If you did use your satnav to return home from your drive, as you have said, we'll find it in the memory. So let's have a look at your satnav record.'

Fayyad stood up. Hayley too. Ace remained seated. He was biting a knuckle, his chest heaving. There was a tug-of-war between truth and fiction. Fayyad had no need to intercede. Clearly, Ace had been lying. His choice was to be arrested or to come clean.

'Please, sit down,' said Ace at last. 'There's no need to check my satnav.'

'As you didn't use it,' said Fayyad. 'You knew where you were going.'

He nodded. 'I knew where I was going. As you would have found out with... What are those initials?'

'ANPR.'

Ace loosened his tie, chewing his lip, as if to snap off the words he might say.

'This is difficult for me,' he said at last. 'It is a sin to lie. I hate lying. This house is too full of it. But you have me in your trap, sergeant.'

'I only want the truth, Ace. Where were you for those two hours? A crucial two hours, which is why I am persisting. The hours when Mo was killed. Perhaps another half an hour is in the frame. Up to 2.30 am, I am told.

Which we hope will be narrowed with the full details of the autopsy. No more prevarication. Where were you?'

Ace leaned forward, pressing down on the coffee table with his fingers until white showed through.

'I was with Nancy Barlow,' he said.

'Nancy Barlow?' Fayyad looked to Hayley who shrugged. 'That's a new name for us. Who is she?'

'The mother of my child. John is two years old. Here, here.' Ace took out his wallet and showed a picture of a grinning, mixed race, toddler sitting on a large ball. 'Nancy, his mother, is a nurse at Newham hospital. She finished her shift at midnight and I drove there to pick her up and take her home.' He put his hands up to show he had surrendered. 'I spent the rest of the time with her.'

'We'll need her address and phone number.'

Ace gave them.

A remembered phone number means it is used regularly, noted Fayyad.

'Does anyone else need to know of this?' said Ace.

'We won't tell them,' said Fayyad. 'But it may well come out in court. If I can ask such a question, so can a barrister.'

Ace nodded, perhaps seeing himself in the box. As a witness or defendant?

'My wife and I haven't had relations for several years,' he said. 'And I have needs... I met Nancy at a martial arts competition. She was the medical aide.'

'That Nancy!' exclaimed Hayley who was taking notes. 'A white woman, long dark hair, late 20s, quite short and slim...'

'Sounds like her,' admitted Ace.

'I twisted my ankle in a competition,' said Hayley. 'She treated it with ice and then a compression bandage. Very efficient.'

'She came to several matches,' said Ace. 'We got talking...' He stopped. 'I don't want Nadine knowing about this. You see where it puts me? I don't want a divorce. But if Nadine finds out that I have a child with another woman...'

'That's game, set and match to her,' said Fayyad.

'I am a sinner,' exclaimed Ace. 'I admit it to you. I have a wife and I have taken another in adultery. I have lied to my mother and my wife. I go to church on Sundays, and I do not confess. I hold back and continue my sin. I give to charity. Many thousands to an orphanage in Romania.' He smiled weakly. 'I am trying to buy my way into Heaven. But what ministering angel will take Judas' silver? I shouted at my daughter, I shouted at my wife. I proclaim my right-eousness to the world. And yet how many commandments have I broken?'

'It is not against the law to have a child with another woman,' said Fayyad.

'Not your law, but in the final court of St Peter...' He stopped, took a sip of water, and seemed to have difficulty swallowing. He took another gulp and cleared his throat.

'Nadine will divorce me. I deserve nothing better. Whether I believe in the sanctity of marriage or otherwise.'

'Will you marry Nancy Barlow?' said Fayyad.

Ace shook his head. 'I have but one wife, I will always have one wife.' He closed his eyes, a vein throbbing in his forehead. 'I love Nadine. No matter where we go from here, what sin is revealed, I love my wife.'

Chapter 37

Jack was by the wildflower bed, so colourful in the sunshine. Blue flowers, red, pink, yellow. And all he knew were the red poppy, maybe a dandelion, and that one was like a giant daisy. Did it matter? The bees didn't know their names and they were hopping from flower to flower. Does knowing the names make you smarter?

He knew the main stars in the constellations. And yes, it did make you smarter. Once you knew them, you could pick them out from night to night. And notice any oddities, like a planet moving through. He knew the circumpolar constellations, knew where to find the Andromeda Galaxy.

Take the names away, and what would he be looking at?

But the garden smothered him, the way he felt in a library. So much knowledge, so many books he hadn't read, he wanted to run a mile. But they'd still be there, taunting him, wherever he went. Just like here, the plants mocked him.

That was the penalty for bunking off school. Ignorance. Though it wasn't a capital crime. He must read. Learn a little. But this garden? This particular one, where a gunman had come in, pointed a gun at him and demanded to know where Sally was.

So much more than flowers, in this place. With the table where he'd been confronted, that shipping container prison. The buddleia jungle where Mia had hid herself. He knew that one now, buddleia. Did there have to be bloodshed for him to learn a plant name?

Jack wanted to leave, but needed to stay or he would never be able to come back. He looked at his watch. He'd stay fifteen minutes. A break from work. He would water the flowers. You don't have to know anything to water. Except that plants need water. The most basic need. It is thought, if life is found on another planet it will be one with water. The liquid of life.

Things connected.

Jack found a watering can with a rose sprinkler at the end, and he watered, taking it from the full barrels. Oh, the full barrels, the stolen water. That would surely come home to roost. In the meantime, water. Get used to this place. It wasn't the garden that stuck a gun in his face.

He concentrated on the plants in pots. They probably needed more water as they weren't in the soil, he reasoned. There was logic to this. It wasn't all magic. Once you know a bit, you can learn more. That's how it had been with building work, and with astronomy. Must be the same in a garden. But starting was always the sweat. When it was all a jumble.

There are only 88 constellations though, the same as keys on a piano, Mia had told him. Strange coincidence. But there's lots more plants. Maybe if he knew 88 of them... There's a thought. Get a book out of the library.

It was hot and still, just bees in the flowers, a few birds at the feeders. His discomfort made him hotter. Outside the garden, there was a breeze, but the fence kept the wind off and held in the warm air. No rush, this was a break from bricklaying. This was him getting used to the garden. Breathe. This place was not the villain.

Jack dipped the watering can into a barrel of water. Every dip reminded him of the fine to be paid. But it was done. The plants wouldn't care who paid for the water. Going through the buddleia to get to some pots, it had a tunnel through its wildness, he spotted a white butterfly. Jack approached it slowly. Step by delayed step, holding his breath. It was motionless within the branches. Closer, within a hand's reach. And then, it wasn't a butterfly but a scrap of paper.

Jack reached for it and unwrapped it. A torn piece of a receipt. Printed one side: Acebal Dev. The rest ripped away. He recognised it as Ace's company. 'Dev' the first letters of Developments. Jack recalled Ace had told him Acebal was a town in Argentina, a joke he must have told hundreds of times.

On the other side, was pencilled a number: 136. What it applied to had been ripped away. A phone number, a pin code? Jack pocketed the scrap and continued watering. It could have blown across from the house. It could have been dropped.

He had the garden to himself, no one making demands but the voice in his head. So much of what we do is to turn off the censor. Sleep, sex, booze, astronomy for him, work too. Gardening for some. All to take our minds off dread.

What was he doing here? He should be bricklaying. Jack looked at his watch, quarter of an hour up, almost lunch time. He and Mia hadn't brought any. He needed to go and talk to her, they could go to the cafe, though there was a good chance that Nadine would make them some.

Enough watering. Lunch, then back to work. At least he'd survived the garden test. It's not the place, he told himself. It was a man, a particular man.

He was passing the table, the one where he had cleaned the birdbox. Where he'd been when the man surprised him. The surface was bloodstained. CSI had gone and left it like that. It wasn't their job to clean up. Sally's blood remained. A warning. A last scream.

He couldn't leave it like that. Not for Nadine or Mia to come in and see.

Jack needed soap and a scrubbing brush, both of which were in the locked container. There was water though, lots of water in the barrels. There was a pile of sand.

Jack brought over a bucket of water and poured it on the table top. It made no difference as the blood had congealed. He went to the heap of sand and half filled another bucket. He returned to the table, just as the water board man came in.

The man saw Jack and crossed to him. He always had that determined walk, as if he knew exactly what he had to do, and there was no doubt in his mind that he would do it. Attired, as usual, in brown overalls, the logo on the pocket announcing him as the servant of the company.

The man's face was stern. Now what? Jack put the bucket of sand on the table and waited for the blast. Another demand, to top the one Nick had torn up? Or straight cash, right now.

'There was a murder here,' said the man eagerly, as if he was passing on gossip.

Maybe he'd read him wrong.

'Just here,' said Jack. 'At this table.'

'That the blood?' He gawped, and ran a finger through the congealed stain. 'Whose is it?'

'A young girl's, seventeen years old, shot in cold blood.'

The man shook his head. 'Terrible what's going on these days. Who was she?'

'Sally Baldwin. Daughter of the garden co-ordinator.'

'What's a co-ordinator when it's at home?' said the man.

'Well,' said Jack. 'The way I see it, these community groups don't like the title manager. Sounds too straight.' He laughed.

The man smiled. 'Too businesslike. Bunch of hippies. All talk, no one can make a decision. Everyone's equal.' He looked about him. 'Nice little place though. So maybe I am not being quite fair. I like that wildflower bed with the pink campion and California poppies. Is that wild carrot?'

Jack hadn't the slightest idea, but said, 'Could be.' As it could.

'Ox eye daisies and hawkweed,' the man went on. 'The company ran a course on wild flowers. In the evenings. We have a lot of land with all sorts of flora. I went on it. Last summer. We walked along the Walthamstow reservoir banks with our identification sheets. It's a whole new world.'

'Must clean this tabletop,' said Jack, nervous of talk of a new world. 'Before the co-ordinator comes in.'

'That'd be horrible if she sees it. Well, it's horrible anyway. But she doesn't need a reminder.'

'She hasn't seen your demand yet. It didn't seem the right time to show her. Not with her daughter being shot.'

It could hardly be clearer, what he was hinting.

The man rubbed the side of his nose, thinking for a few seconds.

'Tear it up,' he said.

Jack almost laughed as Nick had already done it.

'Murder's more than enough,' the man went on. 'I'll tell the office it was sent in error. We had a water leak. And I jumped to the wrong conclusion.'

'Will you get in trouble?'

The man shrugged. 'Some. But I get on with my boss, I've covered his back often enough. I'll tell them I fixed the leak. And that will be that.' He gave Jack a wink. 'Just don't do it again, mate.'

'Promise.'

Jack held his hand out. The man shook it.

'Best be off. I'll drop in again. Bring my flower book. Check on that wild carrot.'

He turned about and headed for the gate.

Jack could almost dance. It pays to be nice. The elation lasted just a few seconds. A glance at the blood stains squashed it. Sally was dead. A cancelled demand was just a shooting star. A flash in the sky, and gone.

He poured the sand onto the stains. The plan was to scour the table, but he had no gloves. He'd have to go over to his van and get a pair... Or find something else.

Jack tore off some buddleia leaves, and rubbed the sand with them. It worked, sort of. They tore quickly, but there were plenty more. A jungle full. He scoured away; the rough sand searing the skin of blood.

'What you up to?'

It was Howard, the old chap who had supplied biscuits and water when they'd been locked in the container. Still in a black beanie, did he wear it in bed? And a beard like Captain Birdseye.

'The cops have gone,' said Jack. 'But there's blood on the table...'

'Sally's.' Howard gazed at the debris of damp sand and ripped leaves. 'We need a scrubbing brush and soap.'

Jack almost said 'and biscuits'. But this was no joke.

Howard opened the container, went in and a minute or so later came out with a bar of scrubbing soap and a couple of brushes.

The two of them scrubbed away, to erase the traces of a sad history. Utilising the sand, the leaves abandoned for scrubbing brushes, and soap suds; hot water would have been a great help, but they had to work with what they had. The blood stains were going, scoured away in soap and fierce brushed sand.

Jack suddenly thought: Mia, lunch. He put down the scrubbing brush as Nadine came into the garden.

'I thought you might like to join us for lunch, Jack. You're welcome too, Howard.'

'No, no,' said the old boy. 'I ate at home before I came. Thanks, but I've things to do here.'

Jack knew it was an excuse. He wanted to clean the table thoroughly. It was covered in suds and sand. Did Nadine know what was under the foamy coating?

Most likely, but she said nothing.

Jack left with her.

Chapter 38

There was a bowl of lettuce, spring onions, tomatoes and radishes. Just a single bread roll each, three glasses of orange juice, a slab of cheddar, and half a grapefruit before Mia, himself and Nadine. This must be the healthiest lunch he'd ever had.

It was not his place to criticise. Bring your own if you want to do that. But where was the meat? OK, he'd admit, where was the fat, the grease, the animal muscle? This was food for ducks.

They were in Nadine's sitting room. She had moved the low coffee table and replaced it with a folding table. The three of them were seated round it, the lunch spread before them. The police had gone; it was no longer the interview room. The bin had been emptied, the window was wide open. Cops were still on the patio and in the garden, so there was no option to eat out there.

'Might I put sugar on the grapefruit?' he asked tentatively.

Mia frowned. She was into her health kick and thought the world should be.

'I'll have to go upstairs...' Nadine began. 'But wait a sec.'

She went to the sideboard and opened a drawer. Nadine took out two sachets of sugar, no doubt from a coffee shop, and gave them to him.

Dare he ask for two more? No, he'd settle.

'Thanks.' He tore off the tops and sprinkled the sugar onto the pale yellow flesh. 'So how's it been down here?'

'You should see our collage,' said Mia. Her hands were stained with orange paint. Jack quite approved; it showed she'd been working. Her mother would have been more testy.

'I'll have a look when I've eaten,' he said.

'Your island's coming on,' said Nadine. She had orange paint under her eye. It quite suited her. Perhaps another on the other side? She was beyond him. Walled in by grief.

'You seem to have got used to the island,' he said.

'I am sure it will be fine.' She shrugged.

'In six months,' he said, 'you'll hardly remember the table.'

She pursed her lips as if to say something, but didn't. Instead, she said: 'Howard is cleaning off Sally's blood. Isn't he?'

'Yes.' The only answer possible. 'The crime scene people left it. We thought...'

'Thank you,' she said. 'I'll take him over some lunch.'

'Give him ten minutes to finish,' said Jack.

Nadine nodded.

'Sally was telling the gunman that she'd had an abortion,' said Mia.

'Why?' said Jack.

'To taunt him,' said Nadine. 'Silly girl. He's got a gun on her and she's daring him. Thinking it's all show.'

'I thought it out,' said Mia. 'I couldn't understand it at the time. But it's the only thing that makes sense.'

Jack took a spoonful of grapefruit, it had been diced. It wasn't sour, he hadn't needed the sugar at all. Quite nice, he accepted grudgingly. The spread on the table reminded him of the garden. Green stuff intimidated him, but fleshy food filled him with glee. What a carnivore!

'This grapefruit is OK,' he said.

'That's a compliment,' said Mia helpfully to Nadine.

'I'd like to go vegan,' said Nadine. 'I've only got to cut out cheese and milk. 80% of the world's land is used for animals. Either directly as pasture, or growing crops to feed them. It's so inefficient.'

'Cows and pigs burp methane,' exclaimed Mia, 'which is 30 times worse than CO2 as a climate gas.' She looked at her dad, a challenge. 'I might go vegan too. Me and Mum have talked about it.'

Jack nodded, and ate more grapefruit. What do you say to a 15 year old who wants to save the planet?

'Horses for courses,' he said. Which didn't seem quite apt, on reflection.

'They eat grass,' retorted Mia.

'And so I have to?' he exclaimed.

'Enough!' said Nadine, raising a fork in admonishment. 'Stop the food war. Let's enjoy lunch.'

Jack had finished his grapefruit. He took a swig of orange juice, and stifled a smile. He must be glowing with health. But to show willing, he took some salad, and buttered his roll.

'What's the address of the community garden?' he said.

'136 Earlham Grove,' said Nadine. 'Why do you ask?'

'Curious,' he said. 'It's on a corner in the street.' Knowing that was hardly an answer, but he was moving on. 'There's a lot of sky over the garden, with the empty land next door. I wonder what it'd be like at night for a tele-scope. Though there are the street lights on the side road...'

'Dad's got a six inch Newtonian,' said Mia.

'I imagine that's a type of telescope,' said Nadine. 'Yes?' She was putting salad into a plastic box.

'It's a reflector,' said Mia. 'Has a mirror instead of a lens.'

'You could bring it to the garden one evening,' said Nadine.

She rose, the box of salad in her hand. She had eaten very little, a few nibbles of salad. The bread roll was in the box.

'I'll take this over to Howard,' she said. Her eyes were welling. 'Won't be a minute.'

And she left them.

The door closed, her footsteps padding along the hallway.

Jack said, 'How's she been?'

'A bit weepy.' She shrugged. 'I've been a bit myself. And I only knew Sally for twenty minutes. Nadine says she was a vegan.'

A vegan drug dealer, thought Jack. Contradiction in terms?

'Her father didn't like it, nor her granny. They thought she'd grow out of it.' Mia stopped, halted he knew by the obvious. 'Would you mind if I went vegan?'

'Your choice,' he said. 'And maybe I should eat less meat.'

'For the planet,' she said.

'Yes,' he agreed. But actually for peace's sake. He was thinking of his collapse in the garden the other day.

Chapter 39

Nadine returned, but ate little of the spread. There was no point pushing her. Grief kills the appetite. Jack ate as much as he could, piling it in. This might be food for ducks, but it had been a long time since breakfast. It was edible if you pushed it.

After the meal, Mia showed him the collage. It was impressive, but he couldn't quite fit it all together; whether it was his ignorance of art, or it didn't quite fit together, he had no way of knowing. So he simply made complimentary noises.

'Nadine says I can have it. I want to take it to Mum's. Tell her I did it at school,' she said.

He wondered whether Alison would see through that tale. Fairly soon, she'd have to be told what had happened in the garden. There was going to be an inquest, then the trial of Kingsley Dayville, once they picked him up, with Mia as a key witness. Couldn't be evaded much longer. Alison would have to be told.

When she was out of hospital.

Had to be done. Just not today.

Back in the upstairs kitchen, he got back to work. Almost immediately he felt peckish, like after a four course Chinese meal. You're full when you leave the restaurant, but an hour later you're hungry. It can't be real, he thought. His stomach was full of vitamins and fibre, all that green mush.

Habit.

He was hooked on meat; that was the gory tale. He had the hunter gene, got to kill to eat.

An addictive personality, a doctor had said. It registered. He was always falling in love, and there had been his alcoholic days. Three years back, he'd forsworn the demon. Keeping to it. Mostly.

It was habit; holding him in its grip. Max, the leader at his Alcohol Halt group, said new habits must be formed. Every outing, football game, or party didn't need an alcoholic drink.

Every meal didn't need a slab of meat.

To be considered.

Jack brought in more bricks with the bucket. He made up fresh mortar. Before lunch, he'd got into a rhythm. Fill all the frogs on a course with mortar, flatten it to the right thickness, give it a chop with the trowel. Then go along laying brick by brick. Once the course is laid, test with the spirit level, and knock down any high bricks with the trowel end.

And onto the next course.

Lunch had broken the pattern, but he was soon back into it, working almost automatically, like a regular bricklayer. Brick after brick, round the island.

Fayyad came in.

'Left my pen behind,' he said, indicating the wine coloured fountain pen in his breast pocket. 'Birthday present. My wife would have killed me. Gold nib. I'm going to lose it one day.'

Jack paused. Mortar is useable for a couple of hours, but he mustn't have too many interruptions or he'd lose his rhythm. And speed of laying. There was Ace to satisfy.

'Did you find out where Ace was for those two hours?' he said.

'Yes. He has a second family.'

'The old goat,' said Jack with a smirk. 'Not quite as holy as he makes out.'

'A two year old child, the mother's a nurse. The child stays with the grandmother when the mother's on duty. It checks out. Nancy Barlow, her name. She says Ace was there. But he's not totally off the hook. There's still half an hour in which he could have done it. When he got back to the house, Nick says Ace was in the kitchen for quarter of an hour. Could have slipped out onto the patio and done the dirty work.'

Fayyad was looking at the island as he spoke. It was over halfway up. Inside the brickwork, the hollow middle, were blobs of cement that had fallen onto the plastic sheet. Jack had left them as they were difficult to reach with the growing height of bricks. And what did they matter? No one would see them once the work was done.

'That's a lovely red brick,' said Fayyad. 'I've a camellia that colour.'

Jack held up a hand. 'Don't talk flowers to me. I don't know a dog rose from a turnip.'

'I won't come round your place for a meal then,' said Fayyad.

'Very wise. Mia's trying to get me off meat.' He looked about him as if someone might overhear. 'We had a lot of salad for lunch, and I'm starving.'

'No sympathy there. You look OK to me. Tell you what, tell me who did Mo's murder and I'll buy you a triple burger.'

'Not there yet, so I'll have to tighten my belt,' said Jack. 'But bricklaying helps put things in place. You could recommend it to the police force.' He chuckled. 'Gets automatic; your brain ticks away, you could solve a lot of crimes this way, and help with the housing crisis.'

'I'll try that on the chief,' said Fayyad dryly. 'Bit mucky down there.' He was looking in the centre of the brickwork, at the dabs of mortar.

'Won't be seen,' said Jack. He should put it on a sign round his neck. Three people had said the same thing to him.

Mia rushed in.

'Dad!' she exclaimed, then realising her rudeness, added, 'Sorry, sir. Can I have a quick word with my dad?'

'Anything for our star witness.' Fayyad smiled avuncularly.

'Thank you,' she said. She turned to her father. 'I've a text from a school friend. You know Sarah?' He didn't, but said nothing. 'Well, she says a group are going over Pizza Space at four. To celebrate the last day of term. Can I go?'

'What will you say about not being at school the last couple of days?'

'I'll come up with something on the way. Can I go?'

He considered. He didn't want to curtail her, and it was just after school. And with school friends...

'OK,' he said with slight reluctance, 'but I want you home by seven. No later. You are still recovering.'

'I'll be back. Promise,' she said. 'Thanks. Bye.'

Mia rushed off.

'She's doing well,' said Fayyad watching her run down the hallway.

'Not so well,' said Jack. 'She had a nightmare last night, which is why I want her back early. Anyway, where were we, before that teenage interruption?'

'You said you were mulling things over as you laid bricks. So Mo's murder, what have you got?'

'I'm halfway there. Brick on brick. Haven't got it quite fitting.' He smoothed mortar with the trowel. 'Come to my place at six. I'll be done here, and we can talk it through.'

'I can manage that.' He looked at his watch. 'Must go. Got to catch Mo's autopsy.' He gave a vomit imitation. 'I sent Hayley to Sally's but I'm down for this one.'

'Everyone is rushing around here,' said Jack taking up another brick.

Fayyad was away.

Chapter 40

It was a little after four thirty, and Jack was tidying up. The island was two thirds of its final height. Today, he'd got moving on it. At long last. Something to show Ace. Tomorrow, he'd finish off the bricklaying. Jack rested on the broom and looked his work over. Yes, it was a handsome red; he agreed with Fayyad. The brickwork was clean on the outside. Not so inside, in the shadowy depths. Inside were drips of mortar on the plastic sheet, and some, here and there, down the brickwork. So much of building work was about cosmetics. As soon as the marble top went on, no one would know.

But they could see it now. The kitchen was like Grand Central Station, all the comings and goings. And every one of them had something to say. Fayyad, Marta, and Nick had remarked on the inside. He'd had to say to each of them, it won't show. Like it was an excuse. It wasn't. The inside didn't matter. The outside appearance was where it was at.

He was tempted to clean it up, just to shut them up. But to do that he'd have to get inside the island, and that risked damaging the brickwork as it would need a few hours yet to harden.

Jack wondered about the green marble top. How well would it match the red bricks? But that was not his say so. And there were all sorts of greens. Could be a bottle green, a light seaweed, could be streaked or mottled. Whatever it was, he'd put it on top. That was the order from on high.

Every so often, he had considered the weight of the brickwork. The two ends weren't resting on joists, and to his mind should be. Just a slight change in length was all that had been needed. But Ace had been adamant. Having made the plan, he would not alter it a jot.

CSI had gone from the back garden and patio. So tomorrow, he could use the side garden door. He wouldn't need sheets in the hall. Could have them in here, instead of the newspaper which he'd collected up and stashed in a corner. Might, or might not, need it tomorrow.

The kitchen needed a clean up, as they'd be cooking here tonight. No doubt someone would complain that it wasn't up to the hygiene mark. Marta most likely. Too bad. There was only so much he could do. He hoped they would keep their hands off the brickwork. It wouldn't be firm for a while. Final setting took weeks. Just one clumsy idiot could set him back another day.

Paint. He hadn't discussed colours with Ace for the windows and doors. The same red as the bricks, Ace had said. Jack had some colour charts; he'd bring them in tomorrow and catch Ace. The exact shade, how many coats and so on.

His head had been all over the place today. Work, Nadine, Mia, murder. At least, the stolen water was history. One less concern. Painting tomorrow, once the bricklaying was done. Did Ace want the old paint stripped? If it was down to him, he'd paint over it. Just sand down any rough patches. Ace's call.

But he'd sussed Ace. It all depended how you said things. You had to make him think it was his idea. If Jack said, straight out, I think we should paint over and not strip, then bet your bottom dollar, Ace would say strip. Ace needed to win, be the one on top, which was why he was having all the trouble with Nadine. He needed a more docile wife. Nadine had her own views, her own work, and that was what Ace found attractive and difficult. The contra-dictions. The sex war.

Money. Jack had to get that clear with Ace. It was complicated. Part of his payment had been for keeping an eye on Nadine. Surely, that was done with. So what was his day rate now?

Jack was giving the floor a final sweep, when Nadine entered. She was barefoot. He might have remonstrated, saying there could be brick grit or mortar he'd missed, but he knew she was fragile and might break into tears.

Her feet, like her yellow t-shirt, were splattered with orange paint.

'Does that wash off?' he said.

'I don't care. Do you want a coffee?'

'Yes, please.'

Jack had just about finished, with only the sheets to collect in the hall, but he and Nadine were due a chat. There were always others around when he'd wanted a word.

She put the kettle on and while it was boiling, prepared the cafetiere.

'Where are we?' he said.

'Here, in the kitchen,' she said. 'The day after my daughter died.'

Jack was leaning on the broom, halfway across the kitchen from her.

'I was thinking of me and you,' he said.

She shook her head, the bunch of hair behind flicking an instant later.

'There is no me and you, Jack.' She closed her eyes. 'I am not even sure there's a me.' She wiped a hand in erasure. 'The past is the past, it has gone. Dead and buried. I thought once, possibilities of me and you, aeons ago, in another universe.' Her hand went to her forehead, looking into the distance. 'But in this universe, I am here, on my own, existing hour by hour. I can't add you.'

Jack wanted to go. Collect the sheets and leave. Instead, he was stuck taking a coffee with a woman who was rejecting him. Perfectly understandable. He'd expected it, more or less. But it's never nice when it happens.

What on earth did he have to say to Nadine now? It had been easier over lunch when Mia was there. They could talk salad and the collage. Now there was just the two of them, no one to leaven the conversation. He couldn't keep saying, sorry about your daughter.

She was so far away; he didn't dare touch her.

'Ace and I are having marriage counselling,' said Nadine. She shrugged. 'Who knows? It just might work. We are united in loss. Isn't that stupid?'

Jack said, 'Understandable.'

It wasn't. Not at all, but the fight had gone out of him.

'Sally deceived both of us. There's our stupidity on a plate. Ace and I were both too busy. We didn't see.' Her eyes were welling. 'Or more to the point, didn't look.' Nadine took a piece of kitchen roll and dabbed her eyes. 'Ace says we should set up a charity to support families who have teenagers with drug problems. I thought maybe we could bring them into the community garden.'

'That would be a good memorial,' he said.

It would be, of course. Nadine and Ace were having counselling. Jack was well and truly out of it. Yesterday's man.

Their builder.

'I think I'm going to go,' he said. 'Do you mind?'

She was stirring the cafetiere, and turned to him.

'I'm sorry, Jack. But you must forget me. I can't cope.' She was sniffing, her eyes puffed. 'But I must cope.'

He thought of embracing her, but it was such a long walk across the room. She might accept his embrace, she might push him away. What with counselling and a charity and grief, stay where you are.

'It's an awful time for you,' Jack said. 'I won't complicate it. I'll see you tomorrow.'

He left the kitchen.

Chapter 41

At home, Jack showered. Soaping himself, he ruminated, warm water dripping down his face and body. Nadine would be poor company for who knows when. She wasn't the person she'd been. A grieving mother with tears for months and months.

All gone. It would not work. Which didn't prevent Jack's sadness.

Don't go in where you can't get out. Another of Max's mantras. He'd called it the lobster pot syndrome. Better to be on your own than in a bad relationship. Well, Jack was free, a little unhappy, but with no obligations other than to Mia. He hoped she was OK, out with her school pals. Should he text?

Leave her. He'd said seven, give her till then.

Out of the shower, in a clean t-shirt and jeans, respectable and scrubbed, he phoned Alison.

'Hello, Jack.'

'How's it going?'

'I'm out of hospital tomorrow morning. Hooray,' she exclaimed. 'I may be on crutches, but I'll be so glad to be out of here. I am bored out of my skull.'

Jack had sympathy with the nursing staff. His ex could be difficult. And she was going to be more so when she found out about her daughter's activities.

'Do you want a lift home?' he said, ever helpful.

'No thanks. I'll get a taxi. I'll phone you when I'm at home tomorrow and you can send Mia over. Get her to bring her dirty washing.'

'Will do.'

'Had any problems with her?'

Just bunking off school, buying goods with drugs money, and witnessing a murder, crossed his mind.

'Nothing much,' he said, avoiding the hard chat for now. But it would have to be faced. He'd go round with Mia tomorrow and say as much as he had to. Not over the phone. 'She's out with friends now,' he added. 'At Pizza Place, last day of term.'

'My last day too,' said Alison. 'Or would be if I wasn't here,' she corrected herself. 'School holidays start tomorrow. I'll have a week off and hobble in to sort out next term. A convenient time to have a road accident. If one must.'

'I'll pop over with Mia tomorrow.'

'You can tell me all about the murder.'

'What?'

Jack was alarmed. Where had she got that from? Who had she been talking to? And then he recalled telling her about Mo's. Sally's was yet to be added.

'Who dunnit and all that,' she said.

'The cops are working on it,' he said, giving nothing away. 'See you tomorrow.'

He ended the call. Alison was ultra sharp. She'd pick up on any hesitation.

Jack had scrambled egg on toast. An easy filler. Too easy, but he'd had plenty of salad for lunch. Five a day. All that salad, must be well over five. Maybe six or seven, even. Could he take two forward for tomorrow?

He tidied up somewhat as he was expecting company.

By the time Fayyad arrived, Jack was playing with bits of numbered paper on the sitting room table. Jack made tea and placed out the remaining biscuits he had got from Alison. Fayyad took the sofa, Jack sat on a wooden chair. Thinking was easier with a supported back.

It was time to complete the jigsaw. Jack had most of the pieces, but there were a few gaps as yet. Maybe Fayyad had them.

'So what have you got to tell me?' said Fayyad.

'Take a look at this, while I pour out the tea.'

Jack handed him the sliver of receipt. He poured the tea into two mugs. Fayyad was a "milk in first" person, Jack wasn't fussed, but Alison was. A trivial thing, but incredible how worked up people could get over such trivia.

'What is it?' said Fayyad, looking at the paper front and back.

'Ace's firm. It's called Acebal Developements. I found the scrap in the community garden.'

'What's the 136 written on the back?'

'The community garden address is 136 Earlham Grove.'

'How come CSI missed it?'

Jack shrugged. 'It looked like a butterfly in the buddleia branches. They weren't looking too hard. Open and shut case. There's no doubt who killed Sally.'

'Could have been there days,' said Fayyad dismissively, putting it on the table, 'blown over from the house.'

'Not days,' said Jack. 'It rained yesterday morning. This would be crinkly and stained if it had been soaked in the rain. So it had to have come yesterday, after the rain.'

Fayyad picked the scrap up again. 'OK, let me think about it. A piece of paper from Ace's firm with part of the garden address on the back.' He took a bite of biscuit as he mused. 'The most likely person to bring this in would be Dayville.' Fayyad slapped the table. 'He needed the address to find Sally.' He turned over the fragment. 'Ace would have written it. Gave it to Dayville...' He stopped. 'What do you think, Jack?'

'Let's begin with Mo's killing,' he said.

'We reckon the two are connected. But how?'

'Let's take ourselves back to midnight two days ago. With no one dead as yet. Ace goes off for two hours to see his nurse. Nick is the witness to that. He was watching TV in the sitting room. Hears the front door close and sees Ace drive away. Only coming back two hours later.'

'That still gives Ace a half hour window to do the killing,' said Fayyad. 'All he'd need was a minute if Mo was stoned on the patio.' He waved a teacherly finger. 'Try this: combining murder one and two. Suppose Ace, on the way back from Nancy's, drops in at the Shindig. There's Dayville. He bribes him to give Sally a scare so she won't have an abortion. Gives him the address of the garden on this scrap of a receipt. Ace goes back home. There, he's peckish, and goes into the kitchen. He has a bite to eat. It's a warm night, he decides to eat out on the patio. And who should he find out there, stoned and slumbering, but Mo. The man who has disgraced his daughter. The man he kicked out of the house. He won't get a better chance. A slumbering man. It'd be the work of seconds to stab him with a kitchen knife.'

'What does he do with the knife?'

'Washes it under the tap,' said Fayyad. 'Then puts it in the dishwasher. What else does one do with dirty knives? Then he goes upstairs to his room. He has a thorough shower, scrubbing every nook and cranny. And he goes to bed.'

'What about the receipt in the garden?'

'Dayville dropped it, not the most careful of killers.'

'Might there be blood specks on Ace's suit?'

'He's thought of that. Ace takes the suit to the cleaners. In fact, he probably had it in the car when we arrived in the morning. Soon as we let him go, off Ace goes to the cleaners. The suit could even be there now. Might be an idea for us to collect the suit for him. There's only a couple of cleaners on Woodgrange High Street. It's possible we'll still find a trace of blood. Difficult to remove it completely once it has congealed.'

Satisfied with his exposition, Fayyad dipped a biscuit in his tea, and let it soften. 'What do you think of that scenario?'

'Makes sense. Almost.'

'Why the almost?'

'Sally's bike.'

'What's that got to do with anything?'

'It's disappeared. Was in the hall. And then it's gone. Where?'

'You'd better tell me, Jack.'

'Ace was away for two hours. We know that from Nick. Maybe Nick knew where Ace was going. Knew about his second family. People talk. Maybe Marta knew too. Churches are hotbeds of gossip. I was a choir boy.' He smiled at the memory, and continued. 'Let's say Nick knew Ace wouldn't be back for a while. Which gives Nick a few hours. What could he do in the time?'

'Alternative scenario,' says Fayyad. 'Scrub the last. This time, we take Nick as lead. Ace has gone off, so Nick cycles to the Shindig. And finds Dayville... What happened to the bike?'

'Nick leaves it outside the Shindig. The bike gets stolen while he's inside. I noted it had no lock. So in the morning, there's no bike in the hall. Sally was hopping mad about it.'

'So how does Nick get back from the Shindig?'

'Walks or takes a taxi. My guess is a taxi, as he wouldn't want to hang about.'

'That gives us something to work on. Find the taxi driver. Wait a minute.' Fayyad held up a hand of doubt. 'Nick's gone bankrupt. How is he going to bribe Dayville or get taxis?'

'Till money. Nick's bank account is frozen, but as soon as he finds out that he's bankrupt, he cleans out the tills. He pockets the cash. Hundreds, I'd guess.'

'More supposition, Jack.'

'Nick has a spot of oil above his left turn up. Could be bike oil. Plus, you may well have noticed, he's been wearing the same outfit for three days. I reckon you'll find all sorts of debris if you take a close look at his clothing.'

'Like blood specks?'

'I'm saying you might find them.'

'Motive. Let's consider that,' said Fayyad. 'In this scenario, Nick is going to kill Mo and then frame Ace for the murder.'

'That's my thinking.'

'Because he blames Ace for his bankruptcy. Hates him for his wife and kids leaving too. So he wants Ace ruined, as he is ruined. That would fit for a motive. Ace is then prime suspect for Mo's death after what he's done to Sally. OK. Got that. But Sally's killing by Dayville, how does that fit?'

'Nick wants you lot to be totally convinced Ace killed Mo. But apart from motive, it's touch and go whether he'd get convicted. So Nick is going to set Ace up for doing another dirty deed. Getting a gunman to terrify Sally into keeping the baby.'

'Except it went wrong.'

'Nick went over the top,' said Jack. 'If he'd just stuck with Mo's murder, then Ace is the number one suspect. But Nick wants to increase Ace's wrongdoing, so it's more likely he'll get done. He wants us to think Ace sent the gunman. Meant to be just a scare tactic.'

'But Sally tells Dayville she's already had an abortion,' said Fayyad. 'Feather-brained girl.'

'Don't taunt a man with a gun.'

'It never occurred to her that he would kill her,' said Fayyad. 'They'd been lovers. But she'd betrayed him by killing his child, so Dayville believed.'

'Dayville was just supposed to wave the gun in Sally's face, tell her what she'd get if she had an abortion. He was supposed to tell her Ace sent him. All part of the script. And to make sure it holds, Nick throws the bit of Ace's receipt over the fence with the garden number on it.'

'Or Dayville left it on the garden table, and it blew away.'

'Either way,' said Jack. 'Who knows? It got stuck in the buddleia. But consider this. You don't need the street number to find the community garden. You just say where it is: a hundred yards down Earlham Grove. There's no number on the gate anyway. Doesn't need it with the mural on the fence.'

'Too smart for himself, Nick. Out to frame Ace, he got carried away.' He stopped and sucked his lower lip. 'One thing bothering me with that scenario. How did Dayville know Sally was in the garden?'

'Nick phoned him. It goes something like this. Sally wants to go in the garden to meet Mia and get the gear. She asks Nick if she can go, assures him she won't be long, and is not going anywhere else. Nick plays hard to get. Make me a coffee, he says, and I'll think about it. While she's busy, he phones Dayville to say where she's going to be. After the coffee with Sally, he finally gives in. And off she goes. Maybe Nick escorts her to the gate of the garden. Won't go in of course.'

'Possible,' said Fayyad. 'So what do we do first? This has to be proved, not just one of a number of tales.'

'Get his trousers off him.'

Fayyad laughed. 'And the rest of his clothing while we are at it. The oil stain, and whatever else may be there. We'll get forensics working as soon as we've picked him up. While he's in custody, we'll see if we can track down the taxi driver. Then there's CCTV evidence, which may well spot a male cyclist, a little after midnight, cycling down to Plaistow.' He flicked his fingers. 'A man on a girl's bike.'

Fayyad rose.

'Don't go yet,' said Jack. 'There's something else.' Fayyad sat down again. 'I'm sure Nick went to the Shindig. But why go then? It's been bothering me. If he just wanted

208

to see Dayville, he could go during the day or whenever. He needn't go in the small hours.'

'You're destroying your case, Jack.'

'Not if Nick went to get something. He didn't need a gun. He wasn't going to shoot anyone...'

'He planned to stab Mo.' Fayyad clapped his hands. 'Forgetting that one. Nick must have seen Nadine let Mo in the side door. Or how else would he know Mo was there?'

'My thinking too. 11.30 ish was when she let him in. Nick sees it out the window. Nadine letting Mo in the side door. And he realises his opportunity; he will kill Mo and make sure Ace is blamed for it. But he needs Mo comatose to make the job easy.'

'He was stoned...'

'Or maybe he wasn't, or maybe not enough. Best to make sure. So Nick cycles off to the Shindig. Takes him 15 minutes, say. Sure, he wants Dayville giving Sally a helluva scare, but he also wants the date rape drug...'

'Rohypnol or GHB.' said Fayyad. 'The Shindig would have a bucket of them and lots else.'

'Nick gets a taxi back to the house as the bike has been stolen. He knows Mo is in the garden. Still time enough, as he reckons Ace will be 40 minutes or so. So he makes Mo some grub, like a good brother, which includes a spiked drink...'

'And once Mo is out cold, he does the deed.'

Neither spoke for half a minute, contemplating the complexity of Mo's murder, and how it fitted with the crime in the community garden. The timings, the motives, the truth and lies.

Fayyad rose, straightening his jacket, brushing crumbs off his trousers.

'Quite a case, Jack. It fits, but lots of work to do to make it watertight. I'm off to the station. And hopefully, I'll persuade the Chief to issue a warrant to arrest Nick Baldwin.'

Chapter 42

In the community garden, Jack and Nadine were having lunch. A spread of salad, houmous, olives and pitta bread was laid out on the bench between them, under a bower of pink roses. It was hot, and hadn't rained all week.

They were a little way from the buddleia jungle, towering twelve feet high, butterflies flittering in the spear-head florets. Where Mia had hid, where Jack had found a scrap of paper. A long week ago.

Work in the house had finished. The island with its red brick and dark green marble top was a hit. The stools had arrived a few days ago with their green matching tops. Jack had gone on to paint the windows and doors. Once finished, Ace had found him more painting work out on the patio. Now it was all done with. Over the last hour, Jack had cleaned up and packed away. He had been paid, and what's more, most of it had been banked.

He had another job next week. A definite improvement in his economy. But don't crow, he told himself, as you never know what's in the wind.

This was a farewell lunch with Nadine. She was looking better, getting more sleep. Her hair was tied back and she was wearing a deep red, half sleeve t-shirt with a black stencil of Che Guevara on the front. On her feet were sandals, her toenails red.

'We had our first counselling session yesterday,' she said, scraping houmous off her paper plate with pitta bread.

'We managed to keep our tempers. He made promises, I made promises. I told him I liked the kitchen island. It's true, I do. I don't really think we needed it, but I never said that.'

'Are you going to be moving upstairs?' said Jack.

'I like my little downstairs flat. I can get away from Marta. That's what I said to the counsellor: the rot began to set in, when he brought his mother into the house.'

'Will he ever move her out?'

She gave a sly smile. 'It's being considered. Though...' she shook her head, considering, 'that house with just the two of us. Mo gone, Nick gone, Sally gone. And if Marta goes too, there'd be a lot of space. Haunted space.' She pushed her plate aside. 'I can't eat any more of this. Take what's left home. Ah, there's your cop friend. He might like some.'

Fayyad had come into the garden.

Nadine rose and said quietly, 'I feel uncomfortable around cops. I'll help Howard in the container.'

'Hello, Nadine,' said Fayyad.

'Hello, sergeant,' she said. 'Do help yourself to some lunch. I've things to do.'

And she was off.

'We will never be friends,' said Fayyad, watching her walk away. 'Even though she invited me to lunch.'

'It's not poisoned,' said Jack. 'But she has gone vegan.'

'Still looks edible,' said Fayyad. He took a paper plate and helped himself to salad and houmous.

Fayyad was in a bluish grey suit. His tie was light blue on a white shirt. Jack had been shown his wardrobe when he'd visited him and his family in Ilford last year. Fayyad had eight suits. Eight! He had a clean shirt every day, and a rack with more than fifty ties. Whereas Jack would sniff a shirt and if it wasn't too bad, he'd put it back on. He had a suit though, but considered that one too many.

'How's it going with Nick?' said Jack.

'He's remanded in custody until the trial. We've a strong case against him. Specks of Mo's blood on his clothing, for a kick off. And his obvious lies are hitting home. He'd told us he never went out that night, but we've found the taxi driver who took him home from the Shindig. He remembered him as Nick gave him a twenty and didn't wait for change. Obviously eager to get in before Ace got home. And there's CCTV footage, several of them in fact, showing him on a girl's bicycle heading for Plaistow. And oh yes, traces of Rohypnol found in Mo's blood, which accounts for Nick's journey.'

'Have you picked up Dayville yet?'

'We got him yesterday coming out of the Shindig.'

'Couldn't stay away,' said Jack. 'Get much from him?'

Fayyad flicked a disparaging hand. 'One of those tedious 'no comment' interviews. He thinks if he stalls us, he can get a deal. But what sort of deal can you possibly offer a man who has shot a girl in cold blood?'

'A hundred years instead of life,' suggested Jack.

He picked out a small tomato, examined it in the palm of his hand. What had it ever done to him? He ate it, none the less. It wasn't bad, sweet, but how many of these did you need to fill up? He didn't like olives. Food like this always had something missing: sausages, or ham. Perhaps it was like giving up smoking, becoming a vegan. It takes a long time to stop the yearning.

'Why don't you close down the Shindig?' he said.

'The Drug Squad's strategy is to keep it open, so they can keep an eye on certain people.'

Jack wondered whether money was passing hands, but said nothing, as Fayyad would not admit it, even if he knew.

'How's your daughter?' said Fayyad.

'She's more or less OK. It's her mother that's the problem. Boy, did we have a row!' He threw up his hands. 'Once Alison was out of hospital, we had to tell her about

Mia bunking off school and witnessing a murder. And of course, it was all my fault for introducing her to Sally in the first place. Then to top it all, Alison demanded that the money Mia was given should all go to charity, along with the tablet and phone. We've given it to the garden.'

Fayyad laughed. 'She'd make a tough judge, your ex.'

'I can't say she's wrong,' said Jack. 'But I'm glad she did it rather than me.'

'Hard cop, soft cop,' said Fayyad, filling a pitta bread with houmous, salad and a line of black olives. 'It's OK, this grub.'

'Jack!' came a call.

It was Howard, waving by the entrance of the container. A hot day, but still wearing his black beanie.

'They've set something up for me,' said Jack. 'I'm not supposed to know what it is. But I do. Back in a few minutes.'

Jack left him and joined Howard at the entrance of the container.

Much of the inside had been cleared to the side. About halfway down, from side to side, a white sheet was hanging from top to bottom, held in place by masking tape.

'You and Nadine go in,' said Howard.

He reminded Jack of Gandalf with his grey beard and thick eyebrows. And mischievous grin.

'Last time I went in,' said Jack, 'I had biscuits...'

He stopped as Nadine entered, as he'd been about to add there had been a man outside with a gun. An unsuitable reminder for a grieving mother.

'One of you on each side,' said Howard indicating with his arms, 'so you don't block the light. Ready?'

'We're ready,' said Nadine.

'Then I'll close up.'

Jack watched the door swing shut, the light being locked out with a heavy clang. Darkness, like the tunnel of love, but without the beloved. She was six feet away and he would make no moves. Gone with the light. But not quite all. There was a tiny circle in the centre of the door. The one he'd bashed through with the hammer just over a week ago, to get a phone signal. That hadn't been needed anyway as his daughter had beat him to it.

Jack turned to face the sheet.

'Stay on your side,' commanded Nadine.

Jack had no intention of moving. A week ago, in the dark, who knows? But all had changed. She was mourning, she was having relationship counselling.

Just good friends, as they say.

As his eyes got used to the dark, he could just make out the silhouette of Nadine. But there, yes, he could see it, faint on the sheet, the upside down image. The cloudy sky at the bottom, the buddleia jungle coming out of it in sprays. In the foreground was an upside down table and chairs, and in front was Howard. It was as if he was standing on his head, legs astride and arms wide for effect.

Jack's phone rang and he took it out of his pocket.

'Turn it off, turn it off,' yelled Nadine.

Jack glanced at the text:

I'll be at the Pizza Place at eight tomorrow. Looking forward to it. Penny.

He switched off the phone and went back to the upside down pinhole image of the community garden. Weird to be inside a camera.

'We should charge for this,' Nadine said.

Thank you!

I am grateful to every reader who finishes one of my novels. I have taken you on a journey which I hope you have enjoyed. There are plenty of things you could have been doing, other than reading this book. So, thank you for your time.

If you liked *Jack in the Garden,* here's what you can do next:

I'd appreciate a review on Amazon. In that way, you can help me tell other readers about my books. Without reviews authors get few sales on Amazon. So I'd be grateful for your review to help this series get on the move.

You can get a FREE ebook of *Murder at Any Price* if you sign up for my readers' list. You may give it to a friend if you wish. When you sign up for my readers' list you will receive my regular newsletter. This will give you news about me, what I'm reading, and tell you about my future books, PLUS a variety of giveaways.

Sign up at my website:

DerekSmithWriter.com

I should apologise to my friends at Forest Gate Community Garden, where I am a volunteer. There has never been a murder in the garden. Nobody has ever come in with a gun, as far as we know. We don't search anyone. Nor have we stolen water, even in the driest weather, though we have thought about it.

If you live anywhere nearby the garden, we'd be happy to see you. You can see the opening hours on the website, where you will also find the blog I write weekly.

www.fgcommunitygarden.org

Books by DH Smith

Jack Bell

These are all standalone novels and can be read in any order. They are:

Jack of All Trades
Jack of Spades
Jack o'Lantern
Jack By The Hedge
Jack In The Box
Jack On The Tower
Jack Recalled
Jack At Death's Door
Jack At The Gate
Jack In The Dust
Jack At The Lodge
Jack In The Garden

Other Books

Writing A Crime Novel

Books by Derek Smith

All my books, other than the Jack of All Trades series and *Murder at Any Price*, are written under the name Derek Smith.

Fantasy
Hell's Chimney
The Prince's Shadow

Other Books
Strikers of Hanbury Street (short stories)
Catching Up (poetry)

Young Adult Novels
Hard Cash
Half a Bike
Fast Food
Frances Fairweather Demon Striker!

Children's Novels
The Good Wolf
Feather Brains
Baker's Boy

For Younger Children
The Magical World of Lucy-Anne
Lucy-Anne's Changing Ways
Jack's Bus

About the Author

I live in Forest Gate in the East End of London. In my working life, I have been a plastics chemist, a gardener and a stage manager before becoming a professional writer. I began with plays, working with several theatre companies, and had a few plays on radio and TV, as well as on the stage.

In the early 80s I became involved in running a co-operative bookshop and vegetarian café in Stratford, where I learned to cook, and had my first go at writing a novel. The first was a mess, and, after too many rewrites, binned. The transition from drama to novels took me a couple of years to get to grips with.

My first success was a young adult novel, *Hard Cash*, published by Faber. Buoyed up by this, I stuck with children's work, did school visits, and made a hand to mouth living as a full time author, topped up with some evening class work in creative writing at City University and the Mary Ward Centre in Holborn. A few adult fiction titles appeared from time to time, between the children's list, and I have since been working more in that direction with my Jack of All Trades series.

DerekSmithWriter.com

The book you've been reading was designed by Lia at

Contact lia@freeyourwords.com for a quote

Printed in Great Britain
by Amazon

71649212R10129